Mr Pim

A. A. Milne

This edition published in 2023 by Farrago,
an imprint of Duckworth Books Ltd
1 Golden Court, Richmond, TW9 1EU, United Kingdom

www.farragobooks.com

First published in 1921 by Hodder and Stoughton

A catalogue record for this book is available from the British Library.

Print ISBN: 978-1-78842-451-6
eISBN: 978-1-78842-452-3

Cover design and illustration by Emanuel Santos

Chapter One

Breakfast at Marden House

I

'Tell me what a man has for breakfast, and I will tell you what he is like,' as George Marden used to say, though whether it was his own, or whether he was quoting from that other great thinker, Podbury, I cannot tell you. But the observation would come out periodically; as, for instance, when Dinah had declined a second go of marmalade, or a weaker vessel among his guests had refused to let him help her to one of these nice kidneys. 'I expect Miss Murgatroyd knows best, dear,' Olivia would murmur from behind the coffee-pot, and that would be the signal.

'Tell me what a man—or a woman—Miss Murgatroyd, has for breakfast,' he would say, as he replaced the cover on the slighted kidneys and returned to his seat, 'and I will tell you what he is like.' Dinah, smiling to herself, would beat time with her teaspoon. She had a special tune of her own which went to it.

Much could be written about that great national meal—breakfast; has, no doubt, already been written. We might well spare a page at this moment for a few reflections on the split haddock, that strange, jaundiced fish which swims to our table on a sea of butter. What more earthy, we might exclaim, than the plain or dinner haddock; what more divine than the yellow or breakfast haddock! Why is this strange beatification reserved for him only among fish? Why, to put it in another way, does that young cub, Strange, take the thick end round the shoulders and leave George Marden the flat piece towards the tail? He comes down later than George; and just because he shirks his porridge like the finicking artist fellow that he is, thereby getting an unfair start of us at the sideboard—

But at this point we realize with a sigh how easily we could devote a chapter to porridge. The method of serving the breakfast may define the household—I am coming to that directly—but it is porridge which defines the individual. There are two schools of architecture among porridge-eaters. There is the school which regards it as the foundation-stone for all that is to come, and there is the school which regards it as the keystone of all that has been. Well, perhaps not a keystone so much as a cement for filling up the interstices. It is difficult not to be crude about this, but you see what I mean. One begins or one ends with porridge. George began with it. That he walked up and down while shovelling it away, and denied himself sugar, may be attributed, such is the force of heredity, to a maternal grandmother who came from Aberdeenshire. It was, my dear Miss Murgatroyd, the only way to eat porridge.

George's way was, in fact, the only way in which to do anything. It was not that he differed greatly from other people, but that other people differed so greatly from him. He resented this; it was so stupid of them. George's way, the Marden way, was the happy mean. How could he help feeling unhappy if other people did not follow it?

We are still at breakfast, so let us consider this question of the best method of serving it. I am speaking of breakfast in the country where there are no omnibuses, trains, or trams to be caught. There are houses in which breakfast is as ceremonial as dinner; indeed, more so, for it is intertwined with the religious ceremony of family prayers. At the summons of the gong we hurry down the stairs buttoning the last button as we go. They are waiting for us as usual; we give them a hushed good morning as we take our seats. Now the butler is counting us. We are all here except Miss Debenham, who (let us hope) is prevented by indisposition, not irreligion, from appearing to-day. The butler gives the summons to the rest of the staff. They file in. We look at them with interest, for this is the only opportunity we have of seeing some of them. What a very pretty girl, the second from the—no, no, we are letting our thoughts wander. Miss Debenham appears suddenly at the door, full of surprised apologies. The butler gives her a pained look. Ought we to offer her our seat? The point of etiquette is a little difficult. Fortunately she solves it for us by sitting next to the second housemaid, the one with dark hair, not the very pretty one who—But our thoughts are wandering again …

And so to breakfast—a full house. Host, with dishes in front of him, at one end; hostess, with the coffee cups, at the other. Ham and cold partridge on the sideboard. The gentleman opposite to us begins his narration of the extraordinarily humorous dream which he had last night. There is a feeling that he ought perhaps to have waited a little. I remember, as a small boy, keeping a calculating eye on the grown-up kneeling next to me, and jumping on to his back the moment that the 'Amens' had been said. Strictly speaking, prayers were over at that moment, but it was felt that I had been premature. So we have a feeling now that the gentleman opposite to us should have let the conversation drift insensibly from grave to gay before telling us about his triumphal procession to the Mansion House in the top-half of his pyjamas. He should have waited until he was at the ham-and-partridge stage; might, indeed, have kept it for the marmalade. We should not have complained.

Well, there you have the ceremonious breakfast. We sit down together; we get up together. At the other extreme is the nine to eleven breakfast. Perhaps the 'nine' misleads us on our first visit. Feeling as yet uncertain of the way to the dining-room, we resolve to be in good time for the expedition; 9.1' finds us on the stairs. The dining-room is empty. It seems that nobody has ever had breakfast there, nor ever will. Fearing that there may be some local etiquette in the matter, we go for a long walk in the park, returning at 9.4' to find (Thank Heaven!) a fellow-guest at work. The drinks are at one side-table, the cold food at another; the hot dishes in a cunningly-disposed incinerator, which we might well have missed without an introduction. Our new friend finishes his meal, and strolls outside for a pipe. Others find their way in. The women help themselves, such of them as come down to breakfast. Our host appears last, our hostess not at all. A thoroughly informal meal, with or without conversation as you prefer.

Neither of these breakfasts was the Marden breakfast. At Marden House (in Buckinghamshire) they struck the happy mean. The food was on the side-tables and you helped yourself, but Olivia gave you your coffee. If Olivia were late, George would be exceedingly annoyed, but life would still be possible. Dinah could pour out his coffee for him. If Dinah were late, too, and there were no guests of the coffee-pouring sex available, break-fast would be a dry and bitter thing, a torment to a man who liked his household properly ordered. On such an occasion Brian Strange (it was just the sort of thing he would do) had poured out his own coffee, and had even offered Mr. Marden some. George looked at him in amazement, as if wondering where he had learnt the art, accepted his cup monosyllabically, and spent the rest of the morning on the home-farm in communion with himself. The coffee had tasted just the same—that was the extraordinary thing.

This was on one of those rare days when Brian was not the last down for breakfast. At the happy-mean or Marden break-fast we may be late, but not too late. One reason for this is that though we need not all sit down together, we like to get up together. Perhaps George will push his chair back before the last guest has finished and begin to fill a pipe. Perhaps, if all the women are quite sure that they won't have any more—as is likely enough, seeing what finicking appetites they have nowadays, always excepting Aunt Julia, of course—perhaps he will even light it in a tentative way; which makes it possible for us also to push our chairs back, as if casually and for the greater freedom of our legs. The last guest then realizes that he has finished. Olivia with that dear smile of hers says, 'Well!' and we all get up. The Marden breakfast is over. But you see how difficult it would be for the early ones if people came down at any time they liked. The whole morning would be wasted.

Breakfast, then, at nine o'clock at Marden House in Buckinghamshire, and we may be as late as 9.1' if we like. Well, perhaps 9.20. George may ask us sarcastically if we have slept well, but his recovery is certain. However, 9.20 is the limit. Brian varied between 9.10 when there was haddock (or so it seemed to George) and 9.2' when there wasn't. You never know where you are with these artist fellows; probably he asked the cook overnight.

II

On a certain sunny morning in July, the grandfather clock in the corner of the dining-room had just finished its pleasing indication of nine when George opened the door and came briskly in. A good-looking fellow, George, of the type which you may see in a hundred English country-houses; the type which preserves throughout the longest day its air of being freshly tubbed and freshly shorn; blue-eyed, brown-haired with a crinkle to it, moustached within the limits of a narrow mouth, stubborn-chinned; honest, unimaginative; a gentleman without a surprise to him, and for that reason the better to be trusted. George Marden, forty-two next birthday, five foot eleven for the last twenty-three years, and eleven stone ten that very morning on the weighing-machine in his bathroom. A good fellow, George.

Porridge in hand, he stood with his back to the empty fire-place, and surveyed so much of his heritage as came within view. Often, in the middle of whatever he was doing or thinking, George would rest suddenly, look round him, and see that it was good. As he rested thus, drinking in his prosperity, his thoughts were never very definitely formulated. A glow of quiet satisfaction would steal over his mind, in which thoughts flickered for a moment and died down again. 'It was his—it had been his father's before him—(*Ah, but it was good!*)—his grand-father's—his great-grandfather's ... Some day, please God, if Olivia had a son, it would be his son's after him ... *Ah, but it was good!*'

His thoughts went no farther. He never wondered why he, George Marden, was so blessed, when John Lumsden, who managed the home farm, could at his most imaginative only take a semi-proprietary interest in the pigs, and the millions outside the magic gates could contemplate nothing at all which was theirs. He never wondered, for why should he? But sometimes a frown would draw his eyebrows together as the ugly thought came up that there were all manner of ravening beasts in the world, Socialists and Atheists, waiting their chance to tear from him that which God in His great wisdom had seen fit to entrust to the Mardens. But it was mostly after dinner that he wanted to tell Olivia just what he thought of these people.

His view, porridge in hand, was restricted. The dining-room was there, most of it. He had his back to Anne Marden and Henry Marden (*circa* 1800), but he faced Lady Fanny (1720), who, weary suddenly of the Marden chin, ran away with young Buckhurst to some godless place over the seas, leaving her portrait as a warning to future Mardens to choose their wives more carefully. 'Damn it, but she must have been a beauty,' said George to himself for the hundredth time, and wondered how that earlier George Marden could have let her go. His thoughts wandered on to that Olivia who was so soon to pour out his coffee for him, and he smiled to himself. Lady Fanny was a beauty, but he would back his Olivia against her. He would like to see anybody taking his Olivia from him. He smiled again. Olivia—his!—ah, but she was good!

The silver dishes on the side-table were good, too, and the mahogany, and the widening sector of lawn through the mullioned windows, even the faded curtains and carpet, all were good, and all were his, George Marden's. Thus had stood his father and his grandfather before him, and their eyes had rested upon the same sector of lawn, the same silver and mahogany—yes, even the same curtains and carpet. All had been the same, always, at Marden House.

His eyebrows came together in that frown which Olivia knew so well: the frown which meant that other people were being stupid, or unreasonable, or—not to make any bones about it—wicked. The faint uneasiness which had lain in the back of his mind from the moment when he had waked that morning was explained suddenly. Olivia's curtains! Automatically he walked across to the side-table, lifted the silver covers—kedgeree and kidneys, as it happened—and walked back again. Yes, and young Strange, confound him!

Of course, there was nothing to worry about really. He had said quite plainly that he would not have any of that new-fangled art stuff, neither in the morning-room nor anywhere else, and Olivia understood that when he gave a carefully-considered decision on any matter he did not wish for further discussion. In the five years of their married life Olivia had never failed to recognize his authority. No man had had a more devoted wife. Naturally he had given way to her on certain occasions— occasions when no point of principle was involved—but this was different. She would understand that. No need for him to say any more on the subject. And as for Strange, her friend—where on earth did she pick him up?—well, the fellow was going back to London to-morrow, going back to paint some more of his ridiculous pictures, and perhaps that was the last they would see of him. There was nothing to worry about really.

III

While George Marden is finishing his porridge, and Brian Strange, very much at ease with himself this morning, is sliding down the broad balustrade on his way to the dining-room, let us spend a moment in comparing the two of them. The fact that this would annoy George must not deter us; higher considerations supervene.

At twenty-four we have made up our mind about the world. On all questions of art and ethics and politics Brian held opinions as decided as those of George. One difference between them was that George had remained of the same opinion from twenty-two to forty-two, whereas Brian at forty-two would realize how very young he had been twenty years earlier. This difference was more fundamental than the difference (say) between Brian's vision of a new world, in which all had equal opportunities, and George's reverence of the old world, in which Hodge's opportunity of remaining Hodge was equivalent to Marden's of remaining Marden, or than the difference in their emotions when they looked upon the same painting or read the same book. But what divided them most of all was their attitude to other people's opinions and emotions. George resented Brian's outlook, as he resented the outlook of everybody who differed from him; Brian was undisturbed by George's politics and ideas of art, as he was undisturbed by the opinions of all the other Georges in the world. This was not because Brian was more tolerant, more what we call broadminded, than George, but because he felt, to put it plainly, that 'if the other fellow really thought like that, then it obviously didn't matter much *what* he thought.' The fellow, in fact, was negligible. In Brian's world many people were negligible; in George's world, none was negligible, for even the stupidest had a soul to be saved.

Enter, then, that lost sheep, Brian Strange. Perhaps his hair was a little longer, his tie a little more emotional, than George would have approved, but there was no denying that he was a presentable young man in his flannels, who would be at home, perhaps a trifle too much at home, in any company.

As he came in, he gave George a cheery nod, and threw in a smile for the sunny morning that it was.

'Good morning,' said George. 'Up early this morning, aren't you?'

'Lord, I've been up ages. Getting an appetite.' He took the covers off the dishes. 'Kedgeree and kidneys. I love my love with a K, because she's kind—no, kissable. I hate her because—because she has a sportico house at South Kensington, she lives on kedgeree and kidneys, and the answer's a lemon. I can never remember how that thing goes.' He helped himself to kedgeree.

'So you've been out getting an appetite for once. Glad to hear it. You didn't happen to see Lumsden, did you?'

'Lumsden?—Lumsden?—oh, you mean the pig man?'

George frowned.

'No, we didn't see anybody,' Brian went on. 'Are you ready for coffee?'

'Olivia will be down directly,' said George coldly.

'Good,' said Brian, his hand on the coffee-pot.

But it was Dinah who came in. Brian left the coffee-pot and went towards her. George, at the side-table, had his back to them.

'Hallo! Good morning,' said Brian. He held out his hand.

Twinkles in her eyes, she took it. They shook hands formally; Brian had a twinkle, too. George turned round.

9

'Good girl, you're just in time to pour out coffee,' he said as he went to his place. 'Been out?'

'Rather,' said Dinah. She kissed him on the side of the forehead and, turning to Brian, said, 'May I trouble you for a slice of ham, Mr. Strange?'

Brian put his finger to his lips, and shook his head warningly at her. She bubbled over into a laugh.

When Dinah laughed you realized what a pessimist you had been. God was in His Heaven still, even if you only had Dinah's laugh for it. She laughed often; at the most unexpected things sometimes, as it seemed to her uncle; sometimes, as it seemed to her lover—who thought that George had no sense of humour, a feeling which George also had about Brian—sometimes at nothing at all but the joy of being alive. She gave you the impression always of having tried to keep it back until the last moment, when it insisted; as if she were in church, and knew she oughtn't to, but just had to; it came suddenly and all at once, eyes and mouth and chin. Brian tried to draw it, but couldn't. Then he tried to write it down, and said that it looked like pebbles seen through running water with the sun on it, which was much better, though I am not sure that he has got it even now. But there were times when it irritated George, who was only her uncle.

'What's the joke, Dinah?' he asked.

'No joke, darling. Just jokes.' She handed him his coffee.

'I don't know what it is about your coffee,' he said, after drinking, 'but it never tastes quite as good as Olivia's.'

'Of course it doesn't. That's practically what marriage means. Isn't it, Mr. Strange?' She looked innocently at him.

'Marriage,' began Brian weightily, 'is—No, perhaps I'd better not,' he ended regretfully.

'You haven't had much experience of it, perhaps,' said George sarcastically.

Dinah flashed a message across the table. Brian shook his head vigorously, declining the opening. Dinah laughed, and

George, under the impression that the joke was his, laughed too.

'These young men,' he explained to his niece, 'know all about everything nowadays. The callowest young fellow can tell you what's wrong with marriage, and how a mother ought to bring up her baby, and why a doctor doesn't know anything about his business, and how a farm ought to be run. The fact that they've never been on a farm, or studied medicine, or whatever it may be, makes no difference to 'em.'

'Mr. Strange, defend yourself,' commanded Dinah.

'Oh, I wasn't speaking personally. But I dare say Strange knows the sort of young fellow I mean. There are plenty of 'em in London.'

'Our Mr. Strange, forward.'

Brian put down his cup.

'I will just ask one question,' he said.

'Will you pause for an answer?' asked Dinah.

Brian threw her a smile, and went on: 'Is there a single doctor or farmer or father or anything else who hesitates to give his opinion on a picture?'

'No,' said Dinah promptly.

'Then, if a farmer criticizes my picture, having had no experience of painting, I don't see why I shouldn't criticize his farm, having had no experience of farming.'

'Hear, hear!'

'The two cases are utterly different,' said George.

'They always are,' said Brian.

Trouble was now assured. George would explain carefully that although he couldn't lay an egg himself (he always seemed proud of this) yet he knew a bad egg when he saw one, and was perfectly entitled—at which point Brian would interrupt to say that *he* knew a bad baby when he saw one, and was equally entitled—and, Dinah joining in, the three of them would skirmish from one defensive position to another, with no decisive issue other than the emergence of the obvious fact that two of them could put up a fight on almost any subject you mentioned, and that the third made no pretence to be a neutral.

But on this morning the fight was postponed. Olivia came in, and three chairs were pushed back as one, three smiling faces welcomed her. Dear Olivia!

Chapter Two

A Bit of Young Chelsea

I

Breakfast over, Brian and Dinah wandered into the garden together. As soon as they were out of sight of the house they turned to each other.

'Oh, Dinah!' said Brian, taking her hands.

'Oh, Brian!' said Dinah.

'You do still mean it?' he asked, looking at her wistfully.

'Brian! Of course!' She was in his arms.

'You blessing.' On a wooden bench they sat down, hand in hand. 'You see,' he went on, 'I don't suppose anybody has ever proposed before breakfast before.'

'It's much the best time,' said Dinah confidently, 'because then you know you aren't just carried away.'

'I *was* just carried away. You looked such a duck coming across the grass to me.'

'Did you mean to tell me this morning? Was that why you got up so early? I say, *weren't* you early? For you, I mean.'

'I lay awake all night wondering.'

'Did you? For me?'

He nodded.

'You know, you don't look like it, darling.'

'That's because I'm so happy now.'

'So am I, Brian. What fun, what fun!'

'Madam,' said he solemnly, 'this is a very serious step which we have taken.'

'I love serious steps.' She gave her sudden laugh. 'Oh, Brian, aren't things sunny and lovely now? It's all so—so shiny.' She tried with one brown little hand to explain what she meant. 'You see, whatever happens, there's always you now ... Brian, I expect I'm not much of a wife really, but whatever happens, better or worse, richer or poorer, I will laugh with you, Brian. I'll never, *never* lose heart. And that *is* something, isn't it?'

'It's everything,' said Brian.

She was in his arms again. But only for a moment. He stood up, a man, taking life seriously.

'I say, you know,' he began, 'it's no good funking it. We've got to get it over.'

'Get what over?'

'Telling your uncle. I suppose I ought to have told him at breakfast, only I funked it.'

Dinah began to laugh.

'Wasn't breakfast fun?' she said. 'Poor George. He hadn't an idea. I bet Olivia knew.'

'Do you think she did?' said Brian eagerly.

'Look at me, Brian.'

'I am. I can't do anything else.'

'It's wonderful to be looked at like that,' said Dinah gently. 'But do you think you can do it without Olivia knowing?'

He held out a hand.

'Let's go and tell her now.'

Dinah shook her head.

'And let her break the news to George? It wouldn't work. You'll have to tell George first.'

'But don't you see, darling, telling George things first—you don't mind my calling him George, now I'm going to be one of the family?'

'Go on,' said Dinah, all smiles.

'Well, telling George things first is an art in itself. Heaven does not grant it to everybody. Some of us paint; others write books; a favoured few, like your Aunt Olivia, are George-tellers. And why, in this case, when you have one supreme artist in the house, you should want to give the job to an absolute amateur like myself—'

'It's no good, Brian. You'll have to do it.'

'Oh, well, he's *your* guardian. It's for you to dispose of him as you think best.'

'I'll come with you, if you like.'

'No, thanks. I hate being watched when I'm making a fool of myself.'

'Don't let him think you're just nobody, darling. You're very famous, aren't you? I do want him to understand that.'

Brian hesitated.

'I don't say that I'm not going to be famous,' he said, wishing to put the case moderately, 'but just at present—'

'Well, you sold a picture for fifty pounds the other day.'

'Last March. Yes, I did, didn't I?' He expanded his chest a little. 'Not, of course, that money has anything to do with it.'

'It will have with George.'

'Oh? … Well, I dare say I can get it in somehow.' He held out his hands to her. She took them and stood up. 'Good-bye, Miss Marden. I go. Should I return, it will be as your *fiancé*—what a delightful word! Should I not return, think of me sometimes as one who dared all for love. Write on my tombstone, "He told George ". Pray for me on Wednesdays. Tell the little ones—Good-bye, darling.' He took her suddenly in his arms and kissed her.

'Oh, Brian!'

'Now, that's the very last one, until—until I've kissed George. Mr. Marden is in the library? Thank you, thank you.'

He buttoned up his coat and walked off firmly. Dinah stood watching him. What fun life was!

II

It was true that Brian had sold a picture once for fifty pounds, but he had sold it to Lewis Marshall, and the circumstances of the sale were a comment rather upon young Marshall than upon the picture.

Nobody knew old Marshall. He was either alive or dead, had lived (or was still living) in Manchester or Bradford, had made his money in cotton or wool. An admirable man, no doubt; the backbone of England; one of our great merchantmen to whom the Empire owes so much. Peace to his ashes—if he were dead. Young Chelsea was too busy making songs and pictures, designing backcloths for the latest Art Theatre, to be interested in old Marshall; but young Marshall was welcome. He was willing to be taught. He would exclaim, 'By Jove! that's good, that's *jolly* good!' when you showed him your impression of the World's End on a Saturday night. He would say, 'Yes, yes, I see,' when you explained patiently to him where Tennyson fell short of Selwyn Overy's best work, or why nobody read Lamb nowadays. You would promise to take him round to Overy's one night, and he would reply, 'I *say*, that's awfully good of you. You're sure he won't mind?' He would look at your model for the third scene in *Artaxerxes*, and give you in return that silent admiration which, as perhaps you had already told him, was the highest praise an artist could receive. 'I say, that *really*—' might force itself out at last, but then he would remember, and be silent again. In short, he was learning.

It was Poole who introduced him to young Chelsea. Poole was looking for a millionaire who wanted a theatre run for him on the best Poole lines of giving the public what it could be flattered into thinking its neighbours didn't appreciate; at least, it came to that. On this particular evening he was looking for him at the 'Good Intent', which is perhaps not the best place at which to find a millionaire—even Chelsea's idea of a millionaire, which regards him loosely as a man who has a lot of money which he doesn't know how to spend. For this, five thousand a year is ample qualification. Marshall had just discovered Chelsea then—the material, bricks-and-mortar Chelsea—and was dining hopefully, and with the air of one committed to an adventurous career, when Poole sat down at his table.

'Good evening,' said Poole pleasantly, and took up the menu.

'Good evening,' said young Marshall, covered with confusion.

Poole realized at once the possibilities of Marshall, and hoped that he had found his man. He ordered a bottle of wine to celebrate the happy day. As he ate his soup he wondered what he should put on first.

They became quite friendly before Poole had finished his dinner. Marshall was confessing that he had never been in Chelsea before, but exhibiting with ingenuous pride a knowledge of at least six Soho restaurants. To his great delight, Poole only knew five of them, so that Marshall could tell him what a delightfully Bohemian place the sixth one was, and how you saw all sorts of people there.

Poole looked at him thoughtfully, and nodded to himself.

'You'd better come round with me to Addington's,' he said.

Whatever 'Addington's' might be, young Marshall was shyly excited at the possibility of it. 'I say!' he said eagerly. And then as Poole beckoned to the waitress, 'No, look here, you're dining with *me*'

'It's all right,' said Poole, and paid both bills; 'you can give me dinner another night. Come on round to Addington's. You know him, don't you?' Poole knew everybody, and supposed that everybody else did.

'No. Who is he? An artist?'

'He paints. And he's got rather a pretty wife. Everybody goes there.'

'I say, do you think he'll mind? I mean, your bringing along a perfect stranger.'

'Good lord, no.'

So they walked round to Addington's.

Nobody knew how the Addingtons' landlord lived. It was absurd to suppose that he got any rent from the Addingtons. There was a certain amount of money available for the necessities of life—coffee, cigarettes, and peppermint creams; well, there must have been, for no tradesmen gives away these things; but the interval between Freda's last guinea from the Stage Society and the possible chance of another one from the Pioneers was too long to allow of such luxuries as rent-paying. It was true that Tony Addington had been known to receive money for work done, but he had spent it on the materials of his craft two or three times over before he was satisfied with the result. For he had a lavish way with him. He would design a scene for your next play, if you commissioned it, at the cost of (say) twenty pounds to you and fifty pounds to himself—the landlord getting what rent he could out of the difference.

'This way,' said Poole, disappearing romantically into a narrow alley, and young Marshall, following him excitedly, decided to write home to his mother that night.

It was warm inside the studio. Marshall received, as they went in, a confused impression of tobacco-smoke and peppermint and stove, bright colours and people on the floor, eager talk and laughter. Poole called out, 'Hallo, Freda!', shook hands with somebody, who rose for that purpose, and made his usual introduction, 'You know Marshall?' Freda shook hands with Marshall as if she did, and said, 'You know Pender?' whereupon a short, plump girl smiled at him.

'Hallo, Brian,' said Poole. 'I say, Freda, where are the peppermint creams?'

'Here you are,' said Brian, producing them from beneath several cushions.

'Good! Have one?' he said, turning back to Marshall, and then, his mouth full, 'You know Strange?'

'Hallo!' said Brian cheerily.

It was easily the best evening young Marshall had yet had in London. They were so friendly; they took him so much for granted. The way they talked of money fascinated while it frightened him. They didn't seem to think it mattered. How different from the men he had known in Manchester! He would certainly write to his mother when he got back to the 'Savoy' that night. And to think that he had nearly gone to that Gaiety piece again. What he might have missed!

He sat uncomfortably on the divan, drinking his coffee, and smoking a pipe if they didn't mind; listening in bewilderment to their conversation (what a lot of people he didn't know!), but nodding occasionally to show he was not being left out of it; and feeling more earnestly every minute that these were the people who really lived, and that he with his money—no, not even his own money, his father's money—was of no account in the world that mattered. And Ruth Pender liked him for his fresh round face, and asked him to pass the cigarettes. A great evening.

It was getting on for midnight when he realized that even his despised wealth had its privilege. Addington, a dark gipsy-looking little man, was showing Poole his latest picture, and Poole was saying that it wasn't bad.

'It's more than not bad—for Tony, I mean,' said Brian. 'It's about the best thing he's done.' He turned to the perspiring Marshall. 'Don't you agree?'

'It's awfully good,' said young Marshall fervently.

'I'll hang it up in my theatre, if you like to give it to me,' said Poole seriously. 'It would be a good advertisement for you.'

'Thanks, but I shall be dead by then.'

'I say,' burst in young Marshall, suddenly inspired, 'I like it awfully. Could I—could I buy it?'

There was an awkward silence. Poole mentally decided to start with a Shakespeare revival. He had been right; this was his man. The others looked at the stranger with amazement. He was not one of them; he was one of those odd people with money.

'Do you really like it?' said Addington. 'I mean, as much as that?'

'Rather! What are they—I mean, how much—'

'You don't paint or do anything yourself?'

'Only spend money,' said Marshall, with his shy laugh. 'You see, my father—'

Well, of course, you can have it if you like. If you really want it.'

'Thanks awfully. It's awfully decent of you. If I can have it for fifty pounds—'

Brian began a long whistle of amazement, but managed to change it into the beginning of a tune of his own composition. He took Freda on one side.

'I say, where did Poole find him?' he whispered. Freda shook her head.

'Look here, be a sport, Freda, and tell him that I paint, too. Tell him that I paint much better than Tony. Explain to him that I'm just beginning where Tony leaves off. Fifty pounds! Good lord! Freda, you can't keep a man like that private. You must distribute him. I bet Poole has a first cut.'

And Freda was a sport. Half an hour later they were in Brian's studio; and young Marshall, who thought that all pictures by living painters were the same price, was offering fifty pounds for 'The World's End: Saturday Night.'

'And worth it,' said Poole, who had a great admiration for Brian.

Marshall agreed fervently.

III

George was reading *The Times* in the library. To a patriotic Englishman the papers were distressing reading in these days. There was so much unrest, so much discontent. Why couldn't people settle down happily, as George had done, into that state of life to which it had pleased God to call them? Strikes! Class set against class! Did George feel any grievance against the labourer working in his fields? No! Then why should the labourer feel any grievance against George? Was not George friendly, affable, to the porters who touched their hats to him at the stations; did he not return their salutes with a nod and a greeting? Certainly he did. Then why should these agitators stir them up against him, who had never done them any wrong? The world was topsy-turvy these days. Everybody thought himself as good as the next man. Look at that fellow Strange!

The library at Marden House saw a good deal of George in this mood. On the shelves round the room masterpieces of every age offered themselves to him, but a healthy man has little time to fritter away on reading, other than his daily duty to *The Times* and his weekly duty to *Punch* and *The Field*. Novels were for invalids, poetry for young girls. Thank God he was still fit, and wanted nothing to send him to sleep at nights. No signs of gout yet, either. Poor Uncle John! What a time Aunt Julia had had with him.

Brian came in, and George looked up impatiently from the leading article.

'Yes?' he said.

Brian pulled at his tie.

'Are you busy, sir?' he began nervously.

The 'sir' mollified George. It was thus that, at Brian's age, he had addressed the elder men at his father's table. Perhaps some of the elder men thought that, dammit, they were not so old as that, but George made no such qualifications. He was in the forties, Brian in the twenties; youth must always respect middle age, as middle age respected old age. It was the only basis of a stable society.

George put down his paper and got up.

'I was just going down to the farm,' he said. 'Care to come?'

'Right,' said Brian eagerly. He felt that it would be easier in the open air. Interviewing Uncle George in the library was too much like a set performance, a humorous situation in some appalling comic paper. Why were the most beautiful things in the world—Birth and Love—vulgarized so horribly? A funny man on the stage of a music-hall had only to mention that his wife had had a baby, and the audience was in shrieks of laughter; the whole building rocked at the humour of a woman sitting up with a poker for the husband who reeled home at midnight. Three thousand people rocking with laughter—did none of them get more from marriage than that, did none of them expect more? Oh, Dinah, Dinah, how different it will be with us!

'Did you have a look at the pigs this morning?' said George, as they started off.

Brian woke up from his dream with a start, and said that he hadn't, no.

'Well, come and have a look at 'em. We'll find Lumsden there, I expect.'

Brian cleared his throat.

'As a matter of fact,' he began, 'Miss Marden was out, too, and—er—we—I—well, the fact is—'

'I'm not sure that we haven't made a mistake,' said George thoughtfully. 'Of course, Lumsden's a good man—knows his job—but—' He shook his head doubtfully.

Brian cleared his throat again.

'The—er—fact is—' he began again.

George went on with his argument. There was the Essex White (which sounded more like a butterfly than a pig to

Brian), and there was the Gloucester Old Spot. At mention of the latter, Brian looked up in surprise at this sudden familiarity, but realizing that it was all the name of the animal, looked down again, pondering a new opening. However, by the time they had reached the farm, no new opening had presented itself.

They talked to the pigs. George, by means of encouraging and helpful noises, seemed to establish some sort of communion with them, but it was weary work to Brian, whose 'Hallo, old boy,' several times repeated, lacked conviction even to himself. 'What a life?' he thought to himself, with the happy assurance of his age, and lit a cigarette.

'Ah, Lumsden!' he heard George say.

The conversation became more and more technical. It was impossible to say anything now. They didn't want him; the pigs didn't want him; nobody wanted him. He would go back to Dinah. Dinah!

Chapter Three

Enter Mr. Pim

I

Brymer drove his friend Carraway Pim down to the village, and helped him safely out of the dog-cart.

'You're sure you'll be all right?' he said anxiously.

'Yes, thank you, I shall be all right now,' said Mr. Pim in his clear gentle voice.

'I go down this way.' He waved his whip. 'I'd take you on to the gates, if—'

'No, no, pray don't trouble. I shall like the little walk on this beautiful morning.'

'You've got the letter for George?'

Mr. Pim looked vague.

'George Marden. I gave it to you.'

'Yes, yes, to be sure. You gave it to me. I remember your giving it to me.'

'What's that in your hand?'

Mr. Pim looked reproachfully at the letter which he held in his hand, as if it had been trying to escape him. Then he put it close to his eyes.

'George Marden, Esq., Marden House,' he read, and looked up at Brymer. 'This is the letter,' he explained courteously. 'I have it in my hand.'

'That's right. It's the first gate on the right, about a couple of hundred yards up the hill. He'll put you on to this man, Fanshawe, that you want. His brother Roger used to know him well—the one that died.'

'Dear, dear,' said Mr. Pim gently, emerging from his own thoughts to the distressing fact that somebody had died.

'Let me see, that must have been fifteen years ago. Clever fellow, Roger. The girl's there now. Well, we shall see you at tea, eh? You're lunching with the Trevors.'

'With the Trevors, yes,' said Mr. Pim, seizing eagerly upon a name which he knew. All this about—what did he call him?—Roger?—was very confusing.

'Good. George will show you your way to the Trevors. Well, I must be getting on. Come on, Polly. See you at dinner anyhow.' He waved his whip, and as Polly came on, Mr. Pim raised his Panama hat in a gentle farewell to his friend.

Then he looked again at the letter in his hand.

'George Marden, Esq., Marden House,' he read, and gazed up at Heaven with a puzzled expression. 'Dear me, I thought somebody said that his name was Roger. Evidently a mistake. It is George. It says so here distinctly.'

He went on his way. It was such a beautiful morning that as he walked he hummed to himself a succession of vaguely remembered phrases from what had once been tunes, and his mind wandered pleasantly in that between-land of the wonderful things one seems to have done and the wonderful things one hopes to do, as indeed it often wandered; for he was old now, old in body and mind, but young still in spirit, as young, or as old, as he had ever been. A funny little old gentleman he seemed to the two village boys who were kicking their boots at the side of the road as he passed, so funny that they had almost decided to tell him to get his hair cut, or to ask him where he had got that hat; not that these were the outstanding marks of his oddity, but that they lacked other words in which to express their sense of his difference from the rest of their world. Something, however, kept them silent as he passed them, something in his face, a sort of ethereal gentleness, so that they looked down sheepishly, and then up open-mouthed at his back for a moment, before they returned to their kicking.

Presently Mr. Pim came to the gates of Marden House, and so passed in.

II

'Mr. George Marden?'

'Yes, sir,' said Anne with interest, wondering what it was all about.

'Would you be so kind as to give him this letter?' He held it out to her. 'I expect that he will want to see me for a moment.'

'Yes, sir. Will you come this way, please.'

'Thank you. My name is Pim—Carraway Pim.'

'Yes, sir.'

She led the way through the big hall into the morning-room, Mr. Pim following slowly behind, and stopping now and then in an absent-minded way to look at a picture or piece of furniture which came suddenly into his horizon. However, they got there at last.

'I'll tell Mr. Marden you're here, sir. Mr. Pim, didn't you say?'

'Yes. Carraway Pim. He doesn't know me, you understand, but if he could just see me for a moment—' He was feeling in his pockets as he spoke, and looked up to say anxiously, 'I gave you that letter?'

'Yes, sir. I'll give it to him.'

But he was still feeling in his pockets, and now brought out another letter, at which he looked helplessly.

'Dear me!' he said at last.

'Yes, sir?'

'I ought to have posted this yesterday,' said Mr. Pim, and there was just a suggestion in his voice that he forgave Anne, however, for not reminding him of it before.

'Oh, I'm sorry, sir.'

'Yes. Well, I must send a telegram on my way back. You have a telegraph office in the village?'

'Oh yes, sir. If you turn to the left when you get outside the gates, it isn't more than a hundred yards down the hill.' She went through the open French windows on to the terrace, and indicated the way.

'Thank you, thank you. Very stupid of me to have forgotten. I can't think how I can have been so stupid. Turn to the left and down the hill. Yes, I must certainly send a telegram.'

He wandered round the room, singing a happy little song to himself of which the refrain was 'Turn to the left and down the hill,' interrupting it for a moment in order to look more closely at this or that which had caught his eye, and then carrying it on again from the point where he had left it. He was looking out over the terrace at George's spreading lawns when Dinah entered suddenly by the door and came upon his back view.

Dinah had remained on her seat in the garden, imagining the great scene in the library to herself, until she could bear it no longer. So she went in and (let us admit it defiantly) listened for a moment outside the library door ... *Silence* ... Were they both overcome by emotion?—Or had they merely adjourned to the morning-room? Silence also in the morning-room. She opened the door and went bravely in.

'Hallo!'

At the greeting Mr. Pim turned round and collected himself as quickly as he could.

'Good morning, Mrs.—er—Marden,' he said, giving her a little bow. 'You must forgive—'

'Oh I say, I'm not Mrs. Marden,' said Dinah with a frank smile. 'I'm Dinah.'

With another little bow and a smile Mr. Pim explained that in that case he would say 'Good morning, Miss Diana.'

Dinah shook her head reproachfully at him.

'Now, look here, if you and I are going to be friends, you mustn't do that. Dinah, *not* Diana. Do remember it, there's a good man, because I get so tired of correcting people. Have you come to stay with us?'

'Well, no, Miss—er—Dinah.'

She nodded at him in approval.

'That's right. I can see I shan't have to speak to *you* again. Now tell me *your* name, and I bet you I get it right first time. And do sit down, won't you?'

'Thank you.' He sat down gently on the sofa. 'My name is Pim. Carraway Pim.'

'Pim—that's easy.' She perched herself on the back of the sofa.

'And I have a letter of introduction to your father—'

Dinah interrupted with a shake of the head.

'Oh no, now you're going wrong again, Mr. Pim. George isn't my father, he's my uncle. Uncle George—he doesn't like me calling him George. Olivia doesn't mind—I mean she doesn't mind being called Olivia—but George is rather touchy. You see, he's been my guardian since I was about two, and then about five years ago he married a widow called Mrs. Telworthy—that's Olivia—so she became my Aunt Olivia, only she lets me drop the aunt. Got that?'

Mr. Pim started at the sudden question and then said doubtfully, 'I—I think so, Miss Marden.'

Dinah looked at him in admiration.

'I say, you *are* quick, Mr. Pim. Well, if you take my advice, when you've finished your business with George, you'll hang about a bit and see if you can't see Olivia. She's simply—devastating. I don't wonder George fell in love with her.'

Mr. Pim felt that the time had come for a clear statement of his position. This was all intensely embarrassing. Evidently she mistook him for an old friend of the family.

'It is only the merest matter of business, my dear Miss—er—'

'Dinah.'

'Miss Dinah. Just a few minutes with your uncle. I am afraid I shall hardly—'

'Well, you must please yourself, Mr. Pim. I'm just giving you a friendly word of advice. Naturally I was awfully glad to get such a magnificent aunt, because, of course, marriage *is* rather a toss-up, isn't it, and George might have gone off with anybody.'

Mr. Pim began to explain that he had had no experience of marriage, but that he would really have to be getting along now; at least, he would have explained all this if Dinah had given him a moment in which to say it. But she was sweeping on again.

'Of course, it's different on the stage,' she said, 'where guardians always marry their wards in the third act, but George couldn't very well marry me because I'm his niece. Mind you, I don't say that I should have had him, because between ourselves he is a little bit old-fashioned.'

'So he married Mrs.—er—Marden instead,' said Mr. Pim feebly. 'Mrs. Telworthy. Don't say you've forgotten already just when you were getting so good at names. Mrs. Telworthy.' She swung herself over the back of the sofa and was sitting beside him. 'You see,' she went on earnestly, 'Olivia married the Telworthy man and went to Australia with him, and *he* drank himself to death in the bush—or wherever you drink yourself to death out there—and Olivia came back to England, and met my uncle—that's George—and he fell in love with her and proposed to her, and he came into my room that night, I was about fourteen, and turned on the light and said in his heaviest voice, "Dinah, how would you like to have a beautiful aunt of your own?" and I said, "Congratulations, George," because, of course, I'd seen it coming for weeks. That was the first time I called him George. Telworthy—isn't it a funny name?'

'Very singular,' said Mr. Pim revolving the story in his mind, but feeling strongly that he ought not to be listening to it. 'From Australia, you say?' He knew Australia, parts of Australia, well. Certainly a very curious name.

'Yes, Australia,' said Dinah. 'At least that's where he went. I always say that he's probably still alive, and will turn up here one morning and annoy George—like they do sometimes, you know.' She sighed and added, 'But I'm afraid there's not much chance.'

Mr. Pim was horrified.

'Really, Miss Marden!' he exclaimed. 'Really!' and he held up a protesting hand.

Dinah laughed.

'Well, of course, I don't really *want* it to happen,' she said, and then added wistfully, 'but it would be rather exciting, wouldn't it?' She shook her head sadly at the impossibility of it. 'You know, things like that never seem to occur down here. There was a hay-rick burnt down about a mile away last year, but that isn't quite the same thing, is it?'

Mr. Pim admitted that that was certainly different. Really this was a very embarrassing young lady. She had no business at all to be telling him all these family secrets. Why didn't somebody come and take her away?

Dinah looked round the room to make sure that they were alone, and then put her head close to his.

'Of course,' she began in a mysterious voice, 'something very, very wonderful did happen this morning, but I'm not sure if I know you well enough—'

Mr. Pim recoiled in horror.

'Really, Miss Marden,' he protested, 'I am only a—a passer-by.

Here to-day and gone to-morrow. You really mustn't—'

'And yet there's something about you,' said Dinah, looking at him lovingly, 'which inspires confidence. The fact is'—she was whispering in his ear now—'I got engaged before breakfast!'

The announcement relieved Mr. Pim. Here was news which the whole world would know directly; the engagement anyhow—even if not the fact that it happened before breakfast. He beamed at her.

'Dear me. I do congratulate you,' he said.

'I expect that's why George is keeping you such a long time. Brian, my young man, the well-known painter'—she paused and added with a sigh, 'only nobody has ever heard of him—he's smoking a pipe with George in the library, and asking for his niece's hand.' She jumped up and seized his hands. 'Oh, Mr. Pim, isn't it exciting?'

She pulled him out of his seat. He was excited too; she was so young, so delightfully young and happy. She seemed to want him to dance with her. For a moment he wondered whether it mightn't come to that, as he stood there beaming at her and nodding his head. Then her next words woke him up.

'You're really rather lucky, Mr. Pim. I mean being told so soon. Even Olivia doesn't know yet.'

And he was a perfect stranger, a passer-by! Really, she shouldn't do these things!

'Yes, yes,' he said, looking at his watch, and moving towards the door. 'I congratulate you, Miss Marden. Perhaps now it would be better if I—'

But at that moment Anne came in.

'Mr. Marden is out at the moment, sir,' she began.

'I think he must be down at the farm. If you—Oh, I didn't see you, Miss Dinah.'

'It's all right, Anne,' said Dinah cheerily. '*I'm* looking after Mr. Pim.'

'Yes, miss.' She went out again.

Excitement in her eyes, Dinah came up to Mr. Pim and clutched him by the arm.

'That's me!' she said, nodding at him.

Mr. Pim looked startled.

'They can't discuss me in the library without breaking down, so they're walking up and down outside, blowing their noses and slashing at the thistles, so as to conceal their emotion. *You* know. I expect Brian—'

Mr. Pim decided that he must really be firm.

'Yes, I think, Miss Marden,' he said timidly, 'I had better go now and return a little later. I have a telegram which I require to send, and perhaps by the time I come back—'

'Oh, but how disappointing of you when we were getting on together so nicely! And it was just going to be *your* turn to tell me all about yourself.'

'I have really nothing to tell, Miss Marden. I have a letter of introduction to Mr. Marden, who in turn, I hope, will give me a letter to a certain distinguished man whom it is necessary for me to meet. That is all. That is really all.' He held out his hand to her with a kindly smile. 'And now, Miss Marden, I will say good-bye.'

'Oh, I'll start you on your way to the post office,' said Dinah. She laughed suddenly, and taking his arm, went on. 'I want to know if you're married, and all that sort of thing.'

'No, no, I'm not married,' he protested hastily.

'Well, I expect you've got heaps to tell me. We'll go out this way, shall we? It's quicker. Got your hat?'

'Yes, yes, I've got my hat,' said Mr. Pim, and he showed it to her proudly.

'That's right.' She gave his arm a squeeze. 'Isn't it fun, Mr. Pim? I mean everything.'

He chuckled happily. He was feeling more comfortable now that the revelations were over; and she was so very young and fresh and innocent. They went out of the French windows together and on to the terrace—quite old friends.

III

'What a life!' said Brian, as he walked back to the house, leaving George and Lumsden to the pigs.

What a life was George's, what a life was Lumsden's? What a life, if it comes to that, is the Archbishop of Canterbury's, or the Prime Minister's, or the Attorney-General's! Such lives are necessary, no doubt; we must have bacon and bishops, laws and the keeping of laws; but let us thank Heaven that it is not we who are living them. Above all, let us thank Heaven that we can feel this gratitude for our own lives. Happy was Brian in that he envied no man, and felt sorry for most. What a life they lived, these others!

They would have to get Olivia to help them. George and he didn't talk the same language. Even if he said to George quite slowly, 'I want to marry your niece, Dinah,' George wouldn't know what he meant. They could only converse by signs. But how different was Olivia. 'What a life!' he murmured to himself again, meaning this time, 'What a life to be tied to George!' Most of us have felt like this about our married friends, as they, no doubt, about us; but to Brian the Marden *ménage* seemed peculiarly sad. What a life for a woman like Olivia!

He had made his first bow to her at Mrs. Parkinson's. Parkinson amassed money in the City, where, we may assume, he was something of a figure. He was less of a figure in his wife's drawing-room, but frequently recognizable. 'Oh, is *that* Parkinson?' you said to your neighbour. All London met in Mrs. Parkinson's drawing-room—Mayfair and Chelsea, Westminster and Threadneedle Street. The lions were there, of course, but there was no need to be a full-grown lion; the faintest indication of a roar was enough to admit you. And if nothing came of it, if, as the years went on, the roar faded slowly into a gentle bleat, Mrs. Parkinson would still give you a smile of welcome. She liked you for yourself, by then; or she was sorry for you; or perhaps she felt that it was more interesting to have a representative drawing-room than an exclusive one. Certainly a bleat is a most representative noise.

She knew the George Mardens, of course; that was inevitable. She knew Poole. Poole, who was progressing towards his theatre, asked her if she knew young Marshall. The fact that she could be asked a question like that, and had (for once) to answer it in the negative, meant that Marshall was worth knowing. Marshall, when collected, naturally babbled about his recent adventures, whereof 'The World's End: Saturday Night' was still the most splendid. Here it seemed was a neglected genius; what was he doing outside Mrs. Parkinson's drawing-room? She got to work. A week later Brian Strange was inside, lunching gloriously, and (as it happened) Olivia was lunching too. They sat next to each other.

Even while they talked—Brian dashing off a hasty impression of his life, Olivia listening with that friendly, amused smile of hers—he wondered what this fellow Marden could be like. Did he understand his luck? And who was he, anyway? Chelsea had never heard of him.

'Do you ever come and see people?' asked Olivia, as they were saying good-bye.

'I haven't got a top-hat,' said Brian with a smile.

'That's awkward,' agreed Olivia gravely.

'I sold a picture the other day.'

'Another one?'

'No, the same one, the one I was telling you about. What I mean is that I could look really beautiful for the money, and buy a lot of top-hats, if you would let me come and see you.'

'Baker's Hotel in Dover Street,' she said, holding out her hand. 'Come to tea on Tuesday, and meet Dinah. Never mind about the top-hat. We aren't hatty people. Good-bye. I liked my lunch.'

Smoking a last pipe that night, Brian let his thoughts wander into an impossible future, in which terrible unsuspected things happened to this man Marden: diseases and drownings and motor accidents; and wonderful things happened to himself and Olivia, whereby they remained for ever young, possibly on a tropical island lapped by blue seas, possibly not, but in any case together and alone. Not that he was in love with her, of course, but it made a pleasant dream to which to return every evening—until Tuesday. After Tuesday, the dream took a different shape, no longer impossible. Just Dinah. And now, behold! it had come true. Dinah loved him!

'Di-nah!' he called out to the glint of her dress on the terrace.

She nodded eagerly at Mr. Pim.

'That's Brian,' she said.

Just for a moment Mr. Pim wondered where he had heard the name 'Brian' before. Then he remembered.

'Indeed!' he said politely.

Brian was racing up the steps. He stopped suddenly on seeing Mr. Pim. Who on earth—But Dinah dashed across to him.

'Brian,' she said excitedly, 'this is Mr. Pim. Mr. Carraway Pim.' She smiled lovingly at the visitor. 'He's been telling me all about himself. It's so interesting. He's just going to send a telegram and then he's coming back again. Mr. Pim, this is Brian—*you* know.'

'How do you do,' said Brian in his pleasant way.

Dinah had left him, and was hooked into Mr. Pim's arm again. 'You *won't* mind going to the post office by yourself now?' she pleaded. 'Will you? Because, you see, Brian and I—' She looked across at her lover, shyly, tenderly, and then back with a disarming little smile at Mr. Pim; and perhaps a memory came back to him of somebody who had once looked like that, how many years ago; or perhaps there were no such memories for him now, but only the sudden realization that they were very, very young. For he took off his hat and gave them a little bow, and then in his gentle voice he said:

'Miss Diana and Mr.—er—Brian. I have only come into your lives for a moment, and it is probable that I shall now pass out of them for ever, but you will allow an old man—'

'Oh, not old!' said Dinah impetuously.

Mr. Pim chuckled happily and nodded to himself. 'Not old! Not old! Well, shall we say middle-aged? And shall I ask you to allow a middle-aged man to wish you both every happiness in the years that you have before you? Good-bye! Goodbye!'

He gave them another bow, and ambled gently off. They stood watching him, both a little moved, for it was the first blessing which they had shared together, and when they had waved him safely into the drive, and there was no danger now of his getting lost, they turned away with a little sigh.

'Rum old bird,' said Brian.

IV

Mr. Pim drifted down the avenue of tall limes, picking up the patches of sunlight in odd little jerks as he moved.

'A curious name,' he murmured aloud, 'a very curious name. Tel—something … Now what was it? I shall get it directly. From Australia. Youth, youth! A clean, happy young couple. But she talked too much, the girl. Tel—something. She had no business to tell me all that. Telworthy—that was it! Remarkable how things always come back to me if I give them time. Turn to the left and down the hill. There, you see; there's another example. I forget nothing. Well, here we are. I will turn to the left.'

He passed through the gate and turned to the left, down the hill, under the impression that he was on his way to have lunch with the Trevors. The sudden appearance of the post office reminded him. A telegram, and then he must go back to Marden House again. A charming house. A charming young couple. Ah, youth, youth!

V

'A rum old bird!' said Brian, and he led the way through the open windows into the morning-room. 'Who is he?'

Dinah did not demean herself by answering. She just gave him one long dignified reproachful look.

'Darling,' she explained, 'you haven't kissed me yet. When two people become engaged to each other, they always kiss each other every time they go away from each other or come back to each other. Doesn't it sound stupid,' she added, 'keeping on saying "each other" like that? Ee-chuther. Silly.'

Brian put his arms round her suddenly.

'But I oughtn't to,' he said as he kissed her. 'Only then one never ought to do the nice things.'

'Why oughtn't you?' said Dinah gently.

He took her hand and went with her to the sofa.

'Well, we said we wouldn't again. I mean until your uncle and aunt knew all about it. You see, being a guest in their house, I can't very well—'

Dinah flopped on to the sofa, and looked at him open-mouthed.

'But, darling child,' she said at last, 'what *have* you been doing, all this time *except* telling George?'

'Trying to tell George.'

'Yes, of course, there's a difference,' she agreed with a nod. 'I tried to tell him once that—what's the opposite to a surplus?'

'A cassock,' said Brian, playing with her fingers. 'Or a biretta. I forget which.'

'I mean a financial one.'

'Oh, I see. A sur-minus I should think.'

'Well, I told him that my budget was going to show a surminus for the quarter if something wasn't done about it. It was Olivia's birthday and I'd rather let myself go. But he never grasped the situation properly. We always seemed to be talking about something else. So I had to borrow from Olivia. Go on telling me.'

'Well, that's just how it was. I think he guessed something was up, because he suggested that we should go down and see the pigs. He said he simply had to see the pigs at once—I don't know why—an appointment, perhaps. And we talked about pigs all the way down, and I couldn't say, "Oh, talking about pigs, George, I want to marry your niece—"'

'Of course you couldn't,' said Dinah with mock indignation.

'No. Well, you see how it was. And then when we'd finished talking *about* the pigs, we started talking *to* the pigs, and—'

Dinah interrupted breathlessly.

'Oh, *how* is Arnold?'

'Arnold?' said Brian. 'Arnold? Oh, the little black-and-white one? He's very jolly, I believe, but naturally I wasn't thinking about him much. I was wondering how to begin. Well, and then Lumsden came up and started to talk pig-food, and the atmosphere grew less and less romantic and—and I gradually drifted away.'

'Poor darling!'

'Yes. What an absurd little hand you have! Yes, well, there we are.

'Well, there's only one thing for it,' said Dinah decisively. 'We shall have to approach him through Olivia.'

'Don't say it as if it were a wonderful discovery of your own. I always wanted to tell her first. She's so much easier. Only you wouldn't let me.'

'That's your fault, Brian. You would tell her that she ought to have orange-and-black curtains in here.'

'But she wants orange-and-black curtains. She's bought them. She's going to have them.'

'Yes, but George says'—and at this Dinah stood up, so as to allow herself more room for a hasty impression of George—'George says that he's not going to have any futuristic nonsense in an honest English country house which has been good enough for his father—what?—and his grandfather—what, what?—and his great-grandfather—what, what, what?—and all the rest of them. So there's a sort of strained feeling between George and Olivia just now, and if Olivia were to sort of recommend you, well, it wouldn't do you much good.'

Brian, lying back on the sofa, looked at her lazily with half-closed eyes.

'Yes, I know what *you* want, Dinah.'

'What do I want?' said Dinah, coming to him eagerly.

'You want a secret engagement—'

She gave an ecstatic little shudder.

'—and notes left under doormats—'

'Oh!' she breathed happily.

'—and meetings by the withered thorn when all the household is asleep. *I* know you.'

'Oh, but it is such fun! I love meeting people by withered thorns.'

Her mind hurried on to the first meeting. There was a withered thorn by the pond. Well, it wasn't a thorn exactly, it was an oak, but it certainly had a withered look because the caterpillars had got at it, as at all the other oaks this year, much to George's annoyance, who felt that this was probably the beginning of Socialism. She would be there as the stable clock was striking midnight. It hadn't struck lately, but it could easily be put right; because otherwise Brian, who would be hanging about outside the park walls, wouldn't know when to climb over and force his way through the dense undergrowth to where his love stood waiting. And then with only the moon for witness—

'Yes,' said Brian, breaking in tactlessly at the critical moment. 'Well, I'm not going to have any of that.'

Dinah's happy enjoyment of these romantic goings-on changed suddenly into the sort of expression you wore in church when you accidentally caught the vicar's eye in the Litany.

'Oh, George,' she said primly, 'look at us being husbandy!'

She sat very meek and straight, knees together, hands folded on lap, waiting for further pronouncements from the Head of the House.

'You babe,' said Brian, picking up her hands and kissing them suddenly. 'I adore you. You know, the more I look at you, the more I feel that you are throwing yourself away on me. Has there ever been anybody like you since the world began?'

'Only Queen Elizabeth,' said Dinah, 'and her hair was redder.'

'You don't mind only marrying me?'

'Oh, but I'm proud, I'm proud!'

'We shall never be rich, but we shall have lots of fun and meet interesting people and feel we are doing something worth doing, and not getting paid nearly enough for it. And when they won't buy our pictures—'

'Will it be *our* pictures?' said Dinah softly.

'Why, of course it will.'

She nodded to herself. 'Go on,' she whispered.

'Well, then, we can curse the British Public together and tell each other that on the whole we prefer not to sell our pictures to them, and we can curse the critics, and—oh, it's an exciting life.'

'I shall love it,' said Dinah, seeing it all.

'I'll make you love it. You shan't be sorry, Dinah.'

'You shan't be sorry either, Brian.'

'Good Lord, of course *I* shan't.'

'Ah, don't say that,' said Dinah, suddenly serious. 'As if it were an easy thing to be a wife, and I only had to look pretty and talk nicely, and you would always be glad of me. It's much more difficult than that, Brian. You could so easily be sorry. And when I say you shan't be sorry, I really do mean it because—because I love you so much.'

'Oh, Dinah!'

He put out his hand and she took it, and they sat in silence for a little.

But Dinah could never be silent for long.

'However, the immediate question,' she said, 'is whether George will be sorry. Olivia will be glad because she loves people being in love.' She stood up. 'Come on, let's go and tell her.'

Brian stood up too.

'Righto. I say, I wonder if she really has guessed.'

'Sure to. She always seems to think of things about a week before they happen. George just begins to get hold of them about a week after they've happened.' She inspected him carefully, pulling his tie straight, brushing back a stray piece of hair from his forehead, and exposing another square inch of handkerchief from his pocket. 'After all, there's no reason why George shouldn't like you, darling.'

'Yes, that's improved me a good deal, but I shall never be his sort, you know.'

'You're Olivia's sort—and mine. Well, come along, let's go and tell Olivia—'

'And what,' said a cool fresh voice from the windows, 'are you going to tell Olivia?' And then with an understanding little laugh for all of them—for the lovers, for herself and for all that George would say about it—she added: 'Oh, well, I think I can guess.'

Chapter Four
Olivia

I

And now, I suppose, I must describe Olivia. She stands by the open window, love in her eyes and her mouth, waiting, until we are ready for her. 'What's she like?' whispers my neighbour eagerly. 'I can't see.' I shake my head. 'Listen,' I say. 'The music of her voice will tell you what she is like.' But he persists. 'I can't hear,' he says. 'You must tell us what she is like. Her voice—is it so very beautiful?' I nod absently. I am listening to it.

She is tall, and a woman; and her voice—Yet, if she had no voice, she could speak to you for ever with her eyes, and if she were blind, you could read in her finger-tips what she was thinking. She moved, and revealed the true goddess: a goddess with a sense of humour. 'Devastating,' said Dinah to Mr. Pim, meaning nothing by the word but that Olivia was worth waiting to see. Devastating—no. Olivia devastated no homes; she flooded them slowly with her dear beauty.

She was never hot, nor in a hurry. After his first meeting with her, Brian tried to imagine her clinging to a strap in a jolting tube-train, and laughed at the impiety of it. When he knew her better, he realized that she could do this quite as easily as she could sit in the drawing-room after dinner. George hated to think that she should ever scramble for a

43

bus in Piccadilly, 'mixing with God knows who'; but, being a woman, she liked these economies, and the sight of her helping everybody else on with a smile, and then saying, 'May I really? How sweet of you!' as somebody made way for her, set you hurrying round to see the number of the celestial omnibus on which these things happened.

She had a sense of humour. You could tell her your most subtle joke and she would laugh at it, but her sense of humour was more to her than that. It had been her shield since first she was married, from over the top of which she smiled at the world when it was being bad, and rejoiced with it when it was good again. The world had been bad to her for five years; now it was very, very good; but you can never be sure of it. Whatever came, Olivia was ready for it, funny old world. The gods who sit in the stalls and laugh at the human comedy could never laugh at her; she was so much more at ease than they.

People wondered why George and she lived so happily together. If you were George's Aunt Julia, you wondered how George could ever have fallen in love with such a woman, a woman with a past. Even if you weren't George's Aunt Julia, but still a Georgian, you felt that he had been rather sporting and surprising about it, dashed fine woman though Mrs. George might be. But if you were a true Olivian, like Brian, you gave it up as hopeless. Marry him, possibly—but be happy with him? Never, never, never!

But then Brian knew nothing about Jacob Telworthy.

Well, not quite nothing, of course. He knew as much as Dinah knew, which was what Mr. Pim knew, what George had always known. Olivia did not talk about those five years with Jacob Telworthy. Those were the days when every ring at the bell sent her heart into her mouth, for fear that it heralded the police. There was a day later when the police did come, and again her heart was in her mouth, but this time for fear that they would go away without taking her husband with them.

There was a day when he came back to her, with the air of one who had been at the front for six months, and greeted his Livvy as frankly and as effusively as ever. And afterwards there were days, but not many of them, when he was sober.

They understood nothing of this, these others, but Olivia remembered. She would have laughed (how she would have laughed!) if she had heard them wondering why George and she were so happy together. Happy at Marden House! Happy with George, that honourable gentleman! Oh, no, no, it was not difficult.

Of course, they did not always agree. George, to take a case, never found his Aunt Julia funny, whereas Olivia did. Olivia, to take another case, thought that some of the rooms at Marden House might be a little more exciting, whereas George thought them quite exciting enough. But these disagreements did not make them unhappy. George was not unhappy, because, even if Olivia didn't see it now, a little reflection, my dear, would show her that she was wrong; and Olivia was not unhappy, because when you have spent five years with your first husband disagreeing about the morality of fraudulent company-promoting, a disagreement with your second husband about the humorous possibilities of his Aunt Julia is a so much pleasanter business that it almost seems in itself a cause for happiness.

For the world was being very good. Sometimes on blue mornings in June, when she and George and Dinah walked through the happy Sunday fields on their way to church, the world felt so good to Olivia that her eyes would brim over suddenly into silent tears. Then she would turn aside for a moment to the hedge, saying that she must have a wild rose for her dress, and, breaking it, would wink the tears away, and laugh at herself for her foolishness, and then again for joy of all life meant now, cleanness and safety and rest. And so back to the anxious George on the footpath, looking at his watch and saying, 'Olivia, dear, we haven't too much time,' and to the faithful Dinah, whose eyes were all loving questions, guessing at the tears, but not knowing why.

Dinah worshipped her. As you watched Dinah, little bits of Olivia kept peeping out at you; her way of shaking hands, perhaps, a tone in her voice, a movement of the head, a crooked finger when drinking. Dinah's 'Olivia Mar den' at the foot of a letter would pass anywhere for an original. These imitations were partly conscious, partly instinctive. Dinah was fourteen when Olivia, the pattern of perfect womanhood, came into her life. In the warmth of Olivia's beauty she matured, adapting herself to the new radiance as she grew.

II

'Oh, well,' said Olivia, seeing Dinah and Brian together, 'I think I can guess.'

They were by her side in a moment.

'Olivia, darling!' pleaded the girl, meaning that she was to be loved and forgiven and rejoiced with and helped, all in one smile if Olivia could manage it.

'Say you understand, Mrs. Marden,' said Brian.

The smile came, and Dinah hugged the arm she was holding.

'Mrs. Marden,' said Olivia, 'is a very dense person, I am afraid, Brian, but I think if you asked Olivia if she understood—'

'Bless you, Olivia, I knew you would be on our side.'

'Of course she would,' said Dinah happily, putting her face up for a kiss.

Olivia kissed her. Then she looked across at Brian.

'I don't know if it is usual to kiss an aunt-in-law,' she said, 'but Dinah is such a special sort of niece that—' She waited, her cheek towards him.

'I say, you *are* in luck to-day, Brian,' said Dinah, almost enviously.

Olivia laughed, but Brian took his kiss solemnly with the air of one stepping into a cathedral.

'And how many people have been told the good news?'

'Well, nobody yet.'

'Except Mr. Pim,' put in Dinah.

'Oh, does *he* know? I thought he was just congratulating us generally.'

'Who's Mr. Pim?'

'Oh, he just happened,' explained Dinah casually.

One adorable gift which Olivia had was that of knowing what questions to ask, and when to ask them. Suppose that you had been playing cricket all day and took her in to dinner in the evening, she might ask you what you had been doing. 'Playing cricket,' you would answer. Some women might then begin to talk about the parliamentary situation, or the price of jumpers, uninspiring subjects to a man who has made fifty that afternoon. Other women might ask at once, 'How many did you make?'—a maddening question to a man who was bowled first ball. But Olivia would know. She would know from your voice whether you wanted the subject pursued or left alone. You were always safe with her.

So being the least curious person in the world when curiosity was not wanted, she dropped Mr. Pim with a little smile, and moved across the room to the oak-chest opposite. And from the chest she drew a pile of orange-and-black curtains, and a work-box.

These were the curtains which had brought the frown to George's brow at the breakfast-table that morning.

III

The faded pink curtains in the morning-room had hung there for generations. They were of that distressing material (you can't get it nowadays, luckily) which never wears out; in an earlier age they made nothing else. If Charles the First, instead of hiding in an oak-tree, had hidden behind curtains, as is much more usual in fiction, there would be as many country-houses to claim that theirs were the historic curtains as there are country-sides to claim that theirs is the historic oak. The Marden House curtains were well qualified. Alfred behind them would have been—indeed, probably was—quite safe from the Danes.

But the fact that Alfred or Charles had found them good cover, or even that George's grandmother had liked them once, brought no comfort to Olivia. Even if she had chosen them herself, a perquisite of marriage which surely every woman can demand, she would have wanted now to choose them again; all the more did she want it, having had no word in the original choice.

For the morning-room was, of all others, her room. She had, perhaps, no legal rights; she had acquired it, much as George's ancestors, one gathers, had acquired the outlying parts of George's land: insidiously. An accident becomes a privilege, a privilege becomes a custom, a custom becomes a right. However it had happened, it was now her room, the room in which she lived, and now, at last, it was to be taken in hand.

'I say!' said Dinah excitedly. 'Are those *the* curtains?'

You gather that, even in their unfinished state, they had made a certain amount of history. George's disapproval had already been recorded.

'I say! Then you are going to have them after all?'

'After all what?' said Olivia in surprise. 'But I decided on them long ago.' As she threaded her needle she said to Brian, 'You haven't told George yet?'

'Well, no,' said Brian. 'I began to, you know, but I never got any farther then 'Oh—er—there's just—er—'

'George would talk about pigs all the time.'

'I think it was a pig morning,' explained Brian, wishing to excuse George to his wife.

'Well, I suppose you want me to help you.'

They were round her on the sofa at once.

'Do, darling,' said Dinah eagerly.

'It would be awfully decent of you,' said Brian. 'Of course, I'm not quite his sort really—'

'You're *my* sort,' interrupted Dinah.

'But I don't think he objects to me, and we do love each other such lots—'

'He means me and him,' explained Dinah. 'Not him and George.'

'And I'd work awfully hard for her and we'd be happy together, I'm sure we would.'

'You dears,' said Olivia, looking lovingly from one to the other. And then, 'Dinah means a great deal to me, Brian.'

'I know she does,' replied Brian. 'But you mean a great deal to us, and we should always be wanting you—'

Olivia smiled and shook her head.

'I didn't mean that quite. I want Dinah to be happily married; if she weren't happy, I couldn't be happy myself. I want her to marry a—a *good* man.'

Brian said nothing, but looked at her steadily. She held out her hand suddenly, and added, 'And I think she is going to.'

There was a noise of footsteps on the terrace. George coming in.

Chapter Five

Husband and Wife

I

George's day was not going well. These things happen some-times. We cut ourselves shaving; there is an unwelcome letter on the breakfast-table; an enemy has hidden our boots; a boy cannons into us maliciously as we step into the street; our money has escaped from our pocket and gone back to the dressing-table. We feel that Somebody is not trying. It would almost seem that on this morning Somebody has forgotten about us altogether.

A man like George is never forgotten, but there had been a little carelessness about him this morning. The ease and certainty which usually marked his day had been lacking. There was that argument at breakfast; nobody liked a good argument better than George, so long as the opposition kept to the point. But what could you expect from Strange? Just look at the fellow's pictures! That showed you. And then he must needs come into the library when George was reading *The Times*. As if one couldn't have an hour to oneself after breakfast in one's own house! And then, when he had got rid of the fellow at last, and was just settling down to business with Lumsden, he is called back to the house to see a Mr. Pim or something. Why didn't Olivia—

51

But that was the worst thing of all—Olivia's curtains.

Of course it was absurd to suppose that she was going against his wishes. She would never do that. Besides, he had told her that if she wanted new curtains she should have them. Only let them be in keeping with the rest of the room; let them be the sort of curtains which one would expect to find in the house of a country gentleman. Not this new-fangled crazy stuff, meant for new-fangled people who had never been in the same house for more than five years at a time, people who craved always for some fresh excitement. Look at the stuff they called poetry nowadays! Wasn't Shakespeare good enough for them? *Henry V*, for example. (George had done *Henry V* at his preparatory school, and could still quote bits of it, to the astonishment of his neighbours.) Look at their art—what was the matter with— well, with Sir Joshua Reynolds? What was the whole object of painting? To get it something like the original. But look at Strange's pictures! Like nothing on earth.

It was with this feeling of ill-usage still strong upon him that he stepped into the morning-room.

'What's all this about a Mr. Pim?' he protested to Olivia's back. 'Who is he? Where is he? I had most important business with Lumsden, and the girl comes down and cackles about a Mr. Pim or Ping or something. Here, where did I put his card?' He pulled it out of his waistcoat pocket, and read, 'Mr. Carraway Pim.' He added, as if that disposed of Mr. Pim, 'Never heard of him in my life.'

Dinah called attention to herself by explaining that he had had a letter of introduction.

'Oh, *you* saw him, did you? Yes, that reminds me, there was a letter—ah, here we are.'

He found it in another pocket, and began to read it.

'He had to send a telegram,' Dinah went on, wishing to keep George as friendly as possible by being really helpful. 'He's coming back.'

Olivia looked at George, who was deep in his letter; she looked at Brian, who was standing uncomfortably near the door; and then she looked at her scissors, which were on the table by her side.

'Brian,' she said, 'just pass me those scissors, will you?'

Brian came towards her and picked up the scissors. 'These?' She thanked him, and indicated George's back. 'Shall I?' said Brian's eyebrows. Olivia nodded.

'Ah, well,' said George, putting the letter back in his pocket, 'a friend of Brymer's. That's a different matter. Good fellow, Brymer; glad to do anything I can. I think I know the man he wants. Coming back you say, Dinah? Then I'll be *going* back.' He led the laughter at this happy way of putting it, Dinah joining in hopefully. 'Send him down to the farm, Olivia, when he comes. I dare say he'll like to see what—Hallo!' He had suddenly realized Brian's presence. 'What happened to *you?*'

'Don't go, George,' said Olivia gently. 'There's something we want to talk about.'

'Hallo, what's this?' He looked from one to the other in amazement. His eye caught the curtains, and he frowned. Could it possibly be—

'Shall I?' murmured Brian to Olivia.

She nodded, and he stepped forward bravely.

'The fact is, sir,' he began, 'I've been wanting to tell you all this morning, only I didn't seem to have an opportunity of getting it out.'

'Well, what is it?'

Brian pulled at his tie, and he looked at Olivia for help, and he looked at Dinah for help, and Dinah came a little nearer to him.

'I—I want to marry Dinah.'

George's lower jaw dropped slowly.

'You—you want to marry Dinah!' he stammered. 'God bless my soul!'

Dinah rushed across to him and hugged his arm.

'Oh, do say you like the idea, Uncle George!'

George broke away from her, and strode across to Olivia.

'*Like* the idea!' he exclaimed. '*Like* the—*like*—Have you heard of this nonsense, Olivia?'

'They've just this moment told me, George. I think they would be happy together.'

George seized the opening.

'And what do you propose to be happy together on?' he asked Brian.

'Well, of course, it doesn't amount to much at present, sir. But we shan't starve.'

'Brian got fifty pounds for a picture last March,' put in Dinah eagerly.

'Oh!' George was certainly staggered. It bewildered him that anybody could throw good money away like that. But he recovered triumphantly. 'And how many pictures have you sold since?' he asked.

'Well—er—none,' said Brian, a little awkwardly.

'None! And I don't wonder. Who the devil is going to buy pictures with triangular clouds and square sheep? And they call that Art nowadays! Good God, man, go outside and *look* at the clouds!' He waved at the windows.

A man may be the guardian of the girl whom one wants to marry, but one cannot stand this sort of thing from him, particularly when he obviously knows nothing about painting. Brian was about to tell him that he obviously knew nothing about painting, when Olivia intervened.

'If he promises to draw round clouds in future,' she said quietly to her curtains, 'will you let him marry Dinah?'

'What?' said George, very much upset. 'What?' He wheeled round to her and caught sight of the offensive curtains. 'Yes, of course, you *would* be on his side—all this futuristic nonsense! I'm just taking these clouds as an example. I suppose I can see as well as any man in the county, and I say that clouds aren't triangular.'

Brian made a great effort to be reasonable.

'After all, sir, at my age one is naturally experimenting, and trying to find one's—' He gave a little laugh, and went on—'Well, it sounds priggish, but one's medium of expression. I shall find out what I want to do, directly, but I think I shall always be able to earn enough to survive on. Well, I have for the last three years.'

'I see,' said George. 'And now you want to experiment with a wife, and you propose to start experimenting with my niece?'

This was rather clever of him. He laughed pleasantly to show his approval of it. But that fellow Strange had no sense of humour.

'Well, of course,' said that fellow Strange, 'if you talk like that—' and he shrugged his shoulders.

'You could help the experiment, darling,' suggested Olivia, 'by giving Dinah a good allowance until she's twenty-one.'

George looked at her in astonishment. She seemed to have missed the point altogether.

'Help the experiment!' he said indignantly. 'I don't want to help the experiment.'

'Oh, I thought you did,' she apologized meekly.

'You *will* talk as if I were made of money. What with taxes always going up and rents always going down, it's as much as we can do to rub along as we are, without making allowances to everybody who thinks she wants to get married.' He turned to Brian. 'And that's thanks to you, my friend.'

There was general astonishment.

'To me?' said the accused gentleman.

'Darling,' said Olivia, 'you never told me. What's Brian been doing?'

Dinah knew the answer to that one.

'He hasn't been doing anything,' she said indignantly

George explained.

'He's one of your Socialists who go turning the country upside down.'

'But even Socialists,' said Olivia gently, 'must get married sometimes.'

'I don't see any necessity,' answered George. It was one of his favourite remarks.

'But you would have nobody to damn after dinner, darling, if they all died out.'

George opened his mouth to say something, but could not think of it. Apparently the possibility mentioned by Olivia had not occurred to him. Brian began to wonder what they were arguing about. He wanted to marry Dinah, that was all.

'Really, sir,' he protested, 'I don't see what my politics or my art have got to do with it. I am perfectly ready not to talk about either when I am in your house, and as Dinah doesn't seem to object to them—'

'I should think she doesn't,' put in Dinah.

'Oh, you can get round the women, I dare say!'

'Well, it's Dinah I want to marry and live with,' said the bewildered Brian.

George grunted. He turned away and caught sight of Olivia, who was going on placidly with her curtains, and turned back again with a frown. Damn those curtains!

'What it really comes to,' Brian went on, 'is that you don't think I can support a wife.'

'Well, if you're going to do it by selling pictures,' said George, feeling that he was on firm ground here, 'I don't think you can.'

Metaphorically Brian buttoned up his coat and rolled up his sleeves.

'All right,' he said. 'Tell me how much you want me to earn in a year, and I'll earn it.'

George decided that he was not on such firm ground as he thought. If some fool had given Strange fifty pounds for a picture, then there might be other fools who would do the same. In a topsy-turvy world like this you could never be certain. Suppose this fellow knocked off one of his pictures in an hour—no, that was too much—say, half an hour. And worked eight hours a day. Well, there's eight hundred pounds, provided you can find the fools to buy them. Eight hundred pounds a day ...

'It isn't merely a question of money,' he explained.

'I just mention that as one thing. One of the important things. In addition to that I—I think you are both too young to marry.' (Much firmer ground.) 'Too young to marry—I don't think you know your own minds. And then I am not at all persuaded that, with what I venture to call your outrageous tastes, you and my niece will live happily together.' This was better. He warmed to the subject. 'Just because she thinks she loves you, Dinah may persuade herself now that she agrees with all you say and do; but she has been properly brought up in an honest English country household, and—er—she—Well, in short, I cannot at all approve of any engagement between you.' He picked up his hat with an air of finality. 'Olivia, if this—er—Mr. Pim comes I shall be down at the farm. You might send him along. I expect he would like to see—'

Brian caught him up in three strides as he was making for the terrace.

'Is there any reason,' he demanded, 'why I shouldn't marry a girl who has been properly brought up?'

'I think you know my views, Strange,' said George coldly.

He was on the terrace. Brian and Dinah looked at each other despairingly; then at Olivia. Very quietly, still engrossed in her curtains, she spoke.

'George, wait a moment, dear. We can't quite leave it like this.'

'I have said all I want to say on the subject,' announced George from the windows.

'Yes, darling, but I haven't begun to say all that *I* want to say on the subject.'

George hesitated, and then came slowly back. He put his cap down.

'Of course, if you have anything to say, Olivia, I will listen to it,' he began reasonably. And then his eye caught the curtains again. 'But I don't know that this is quite the time, or'—his voice became a little harder—'or that you have chosen quite the occupation likely to—er—endear your views to me.'

Dinah felt that she had been silent too long. 'I may as well tell you, Uncle George,' she said firmly, 'that *I* have a good deal to say, too.'

Mutiny! But Olivia spoke before George could get his revolver out.

'I can guess what you are going to say, Dinah, and I think you had better keep it for the moment.'

'Yes, Aunt Olivia,' said Dinah meekly.

'Brian, you might go and have a little walk together. I expect you have plenty to talk about.'

'Righto!'

'Now mind, Strange, no love-making. I put you on your honour about that.'

'I'll do my best to avoid it, sir,' said Brian, with a smile.

'May I take his arm if we go up a hill?' asked Dinah, looking about fourteen.

George felt for his revolver again. But again Olivia was too quick for him.

'I'm sure you will know how to behave,' she said gravely. 'Both of you.'

'Come on then, Dinah.'

'Righto!' said Dinah, rather subdued.

They went out together.

But George had a final word for them as they went down the terrace.

'And if you do see any clouds, Strange,' he called after them, 'take a good look at 'em.' He laughed heartily to himself and added. 'Triangular clouds! I never heard of such nonsense. Futuristic rubbish!' He sat down at his desk, and turning to his wife, said, 'Well, Olivia?'

And then he saw the curtains again.

II

'Well, George?' said Olivia, giving him her most confidential smile.

But he was in no mood for smiles.

'What are you doing?' he asked grimly.

'Making curtains, George. Won't they be rather sweet?' She held them up lovingly. 'Oh, but I forgot—you don't like them.'

'I don't like them. And what is more I don't mean to have them in my house. As I told you yesterday, this is the house of a simple country gentleman, and I don't want any of these new-fangled ideas in it.'

'Is marrying for love a new-fangled idea?' Olivia wondered wistfully.

'We'll come to that directly.' He shook his head over the sex. 'None of you women can keep to the point,' he complained. 'What I am saying now is that the house of my fathers and forefathers is good enough for me.'

'Do you know, George, I can hear one of your ancestors saying that to his wife in their stuffy old cave, when the new-fangled idea of building houses was first suggested. "The cave of my forefathers—"'

'That's ridiculous,' he interrupted. 'Naturally one must have progress. But that's just the point.' He waved an offended hand at the curtains. 'I don't call that sort of thing progress; it's—er—retrogression.'

'Well, anyhow, it's pretty.'

'There I disagree with you. And I must say once more that I will not have them hanging in my house.' 'Very well, George.'

At this point she should have torn the curtains in two, thrown them in the fireplace and settled down comfortably to a bed-spread or a pair of George's socks. To George's amazement she did none of these things. She went on calmly to the next ring.

'That being so,' the indignant husband went on, 'I don't see the necessity of going on with them.'

'Well, I must do something with them now we've got the material. I thought perhaps I could sell them when they are finished—as we're so poor.'

'What do you mean—so poor?'

'Well, you said just now that you couldn't give Dinah an allowance because rents had gone down.' George looked at her in bewilderment, at this stupidity. And Olivia was so quick, so intelligent as a rule!

'Confound it! Keep to the point! We'll talk about Dinah's affairs directly. We're discussing our own affairs at the moment.'

'But what is there to discuss?' said the surprised Olivia. 'Those ridiculous things.'

'But we've finished that. You have said that you wouldn't have them hanging in your house, and I have said, "Very well, George." Now we can go on to Dinah and Brian.'

'But put those beastly things away,' shouted the infuriated man.

'Very well, George,' said Olivia in the same meek wifely voice. She rose slowly, beautifully. Beautifully she walked across the room carrying the curtains in front of her as if they were an offering to the high gods. She placed them on the old oak chest by the fireplace. She returned slowly, beautifully, to the table by the sofa; closed her work-basket; moved slowly to the other side of the room, away from George.

'That's better,' he said, a little ashamed of his outburst. Still she said nothing, standing with her back to him, the picture of dignity. Her silence frightened him. He came a little closer.

'Now look here, Olivia old girl,' he said, 'you've been a jolly good wife to me, and we don't often have rows, and—and if I've been rude to you about this—lost my temper a bit, perhaps, what?—I'll say I'm sorry.'

It was a handsome apology. I'm afraid that Olivia had seen it coming from the beginning. But she was properly surprised.

'George, *darling*!' she said, turning round to him, all tenderness. 'May I have a kiss?' he pleaded.

'George!' She held up her face. He kissed her, taking her in his arms.

'Do you love me?' she asked in her deep voice.

'You know I do, old girl,' answered the fond, unsuspecting husband.

'As much as Brian loves Dinah?' she breathed.

He was away from her at once.

'I've said all I want to say about that.'

'Oh, but there must be lots you want to say, but perhaps don't quite like to. Do tell me, darling.' Thus appealed to, George, decided to make the matter perfectly clear, once and for all.

'What it comes to is this,' he said. 'I consider that Dinah is too young to choose a husband for herself, and Strange is not the husband whom I should choose for her.'

'You were calling him Brian yesterday.'

'Yesterday,' said George, making his best point in the discussion, 'I regarded him as a boy. To-day he wishes me to look upon him as a man.'

'He *is* twenty-four.'

'And Dinah's nineteen. Ridiculous!'

The man of forty laughed scornfully. True, Pitt was Prime Minister at twenty-four, Alexander had conquered Syria, and even George himself was standing for Parliament, though unfortunately without success. Yet how little they really knew! How properly is the stripling of twenty-four despised by the man of forty; who is despised (how properly) by the man of sixty; who to Methuselah on his death-bed must have seemed almost an idiot. How wise then Methuselah must have been—and how unfortunate that he left nothing behind him but descendants all younger than himself.

'I suppose,' said Olivia, trying to puzzle it out, 'that if Brian had been a Conservative, and thought the clouds were round, he would have seemed older somehow.'

'That's a different point altogether; that has nothing to do with his age.'

'Oh, I thought it had,' said Olivia.

'What I am objecting to is these ridiculously early marriages, before either party knows its own mind, much less the mind of the other party. Such marriages invariably lead to unhappiness.'

The sun went out of Olivia's face.

'Of course, my first marriage wasn't a happy one,' she murmured.

It was not what George had meant, and he looked across at her: half-apologetic for having distressed her, half-annoyed at being reminded of that early adventure.

'As you know, dear, I dislike speaking about your first marriage at all, and I had no intention of bringing it up now, but since you mention it—well, there is a case in point.'

Olivia sat looking into the past: beyond that unhappy first marriage to the days of her first love. Such warm and gentle memories they were.

'When I was eighteen I was in love.'

Eighteen! A year younger than Dinah! He was twenty-one: three years younger than Brian. Ah the stolen meetings in the warm days of June! ... Faintly his voice came back to her over the years.

'Olivia!'

'You never called me Olivia before.'

'I have thought of you as Olivia—always.'

'Have you?'

'Say, "Have you, Michael?"'

Shyly she whispers it. 'Have you, Michael?'

'Always, Olivia.'

Their hands meet, are interlocked. Oh, the sweet contentment of it! What need now of words? If they could sit thus, always, until the world came to an end! Oh, the comfort of his hand! ...

'I must go.'

'Not yet, Olivia.'

'I must, Michael.'

'You will be here to-morrow?'

'I oughtn't to be.'

'Ah, but you will, Olivia?'

'I will, Michael.'

They stand there, sighing their souls towards each other. Their love is so precious, so fragile, that even a kiss would seem to shatter it.

'Good-bye, Michael. That means "God be with you, Michael."'

'God be with you, Olivia.' He takes a deep breath, and says again, 'Olivia!'—all the inexpressible longing of youth in the word. She smiles caressingly at him ... Then she is gone ...

Ah, how young that Olivia was! It is not the Olivia who is married now to George. She looks back at the girl she was, hardly recognizing her, yet nodding to her for old times' sake, sharing with her the fragrance of those gentle memories.

'Perhaps,' she says to George, 'I only thought I was in love, and I don't know if we should have been happy, if I had married him. But my father made me marry a man called Jacob Telworthy, and when things were too hot for him in England—' She stopped and said reflectively, 'Too hot for him: I think that was the expression we used in those days—well, then we went to Australia, and I left him there, and the only happy moment I had in all my married life was on the morning when I read in the papers that he was dead.'

George moved uncomfortably. Why talk about this fellow Telworthy? That was over and done with. She was *his* now. His! Surely we can forget Telworthy now.

'Yes, yes, my dear, I know,' he said. 'You must have had a terrible time. Terrible. I can hardly bear to think about it. My only hope is that I have made up to you for it in some degree.'

'My dear!'

'There, there!' He patted her hand. 'But I must say,' he went on with a sudden change of voice, 'that I don't see what bearing all this has upon Dinah's case.'

'Oh, none; except that my father liked Jacob's political opinions and his views on art. I mean he liked the way Jacob had furnished his house. I expect that that was why he chose him for me.'

George caught the eye of Heaven and shrugged despairingly over the obtuseness of the sex. Patiently he explained that he was not choosing a husband for Dinah. Not at all. Let her choose whomever she liked. 'So long as he can support her,' he added quickly, seeing that she was about to interrupt, 'and there is a chance of their being happy together.'

'Brian—' began Olivia.

'Ridiculous! He's got no money and he has been brought up in a very different way from Dinah. Just because she thinks she's in love with him, she may be prepared to believe now that—er—all cows are blue and—er—waves are square, but she won't go on believing it for ever.'

'Neither will Brian.'

'Well, that's what I keep telling him,' George burst out, 'only he won't see it. Just as I keep telling you about those ridiculous curtains. It seems to me that I'm the only person in the house with any eyesight left.'

'Perhaps you are, darling,' she soothed him. 'But at any rate, the important thing is that Brian is a gentleman, he loves Dinah, Dinah loves him, he is earning enough to support himself and you are earning enough to support Dinah. I think it's worth risking, George.'

But George was not impressed by Brian's list of qualifications.

'I can only say,' he observed stiffly, 'that the whole question demands much more anxious thought than you seem to have given it. You say that he is a gentleman. He knows how to behave, I admit, but if his morals are as topsy-turvy as his tastes and politics, as I've no doubt they are, then—er—In short, I do not approve of Brian Strange as a husband for my niece and ward … Matches? Ah, here they are.' He lit his pipe, and the discussion was over.

What a futile discussion, thought Olivia. But could any discussion between wife and husband ever end otherwise? Did the man ever convince the woman, or the woman the man? It was as if they stood on opposite sides of a wall, and argued whether the wall was in shadow or in sunshine. Neither would ever see the other's point of view. How stupid the other one always seemed! Poor George. How Brian's pictures must have annoyed him!

Olivia herself was neither annoyed nor thrilled by the great painter's representation of a windy day in April, or—to refer again to the masterpiece—The World's End on a Saturday night. She knew that he was experimenting, and that, both in his experiments and in the discoveries he was to make, he would seek to please one critic only: himself. That was enough for a beginning. What was important to her was that he gave her— she could not quite say how—the impression of being a 'good' man. There was no other word for what she meant but 'good.' 'Honourable' means so little nowadays. The husband who tells

lies in the divorce court is honourable. 'Gentleman' means less.
Oh, the gentlemen Olivia had known in the days of that great
financier, Jacob Telworthy; the gentlemen in the City, and at the
stage doors; the gentlemen who pass on to each other scandal-
ous stories about any politician or actress or public character
whose name comes up at the dinner-table; the gentlemen after
jobs! But Brian was good. He had nice, clean, boyish, chivalrous
ideas, of which he was unashamed; there was something of the
untouched child about him ... Lucky, lucky Dinah!

Lucky Dinah; for what do these girls know of the men they
are to marry? How blind George was, not to see that Brian was
the one good man in a thousand!

She looked at him as he sat there pretending to consult
his diary. Blind, but also 'good.' Narrow, yes; but after the
broadminded men of the world she had known, how safe, how
comforting his narrowness! And yet—once—

'You are a curious mixture, George,' she said thoughtfully,
hardly realizing that she was speaking aloud.

He liked that. Who would not? He looked up at her with a
pleased smile.

'George Marden to marry the widow of a convict.'

He did not like that nearly so much. He dropped his diary
and started up.

'Convict! What do you mean?'

'Jacob Telworthy. Convict Two Hundred and—, no, I
forget his number. Surely I told you all this, dear, when we got
engaged?'

Yes, she had told him, but he had refused to listen. 'What
does it matter?' he had said. 'I want *you*! *You!*' Had she told him?
He had told himself afterwards that she had not. Telworthy
was dead; he had died in Australia conveniently enough. Never
mind what he had been in his life-time. He did not want to
ask Olivia, and there was no need for Olivia to tell him. If she
did not tell him, then there was no need for him to bear the

reproachful looks of those Mardens on his walls, because a Marden of Marden House had married the widow of a —No, she had not told him.

'I told you,' went on Olivia innocently, 'how he carelessly put the wrong signature to a cheque for a thousand pounds in England, and how he made a little mistake about two or three companies he promoted in Australia, and how—'

'I didn't realize he had actually been convicted,' mumbled George.

'But what difference does it make?'

Eagerly he seized the chance of escaping from the dishonest confusion of his own mind, and held up his hands in amazement at the stupidity of his wife's.

'My dear Olivia!' he said 'If you can't see that!'

'So you see,' she went on inconsequently, 'we need not be too particular about our niece, need we?'

George pulled himself together.

'I think,' he said coldly, 'we had better leave your first husband out of the conversation altogether. I never wished to refer to him; I never wish to hear about him again. As for this other matter, I don't for a moment take it seriously. Dinah is an exceptionally pretty girl, and Strange is a good-looking boy. If they are attracted by each other, it is a mere outward attraction, which, I am convinced, will not lead to any lasting happiness.' He raised his hand as she seemed about to say something, and went on firmly: 'Now, Olivia, that must be regarded as my last word on the subject. If this Mr.—er—what's his name?—comes back, I shall be down at the farm.' He picked up his cap and went out.

Olivia looked after him as he strode across the terrace, shaking her head tenderly at him. Then, with a smile, she went back to her curtains.

Chapter Six
Two Children

I

If Roger Marden had lived, George would have been an Under-Secretary by this time, for it was a tradition of Marden House that the younger sons went into politics. John Marden, George's uncle, had gone into them so successfully that he left the Local Government Board with a baronetcy; indeed, had he been only a trifle more incompetent, he might have been assisted out of the House of Commons altogether with a peerage. But a peerage could not be wasted on a man who had been as little attacked by the venal Press as John. True, the more vulgar papers asserted that he was stupid, as if that were anything against a man, but even his political enemies admitted that he possessed that bull-dog British obstinacy which, from the beginning of history, has pulled the country through her difficulties. Moreover, Julia, his wife, had a frank way of speaking her mind at Dog Shows about her friends and acquaintances, which, taken in conjunction with John's red face, gout, and love of horses, created a strong impression that the Local Government Board was, at any rate, in honest hands. And that was something.

It fell to George to continue the political tradition. As quite a young man he had fought his first election, but, owing to the lies of the other side, was defeated. Roger's early death prevented him from carrying on the unequal fight. He returned to Marden House with a small service of plate, and settled down as heir; to the relief of numerous Mardens, particularly Aunt Julia, who saw in him a more suitable Head of the House than Roger could ever have been. For Roger, by the publication of a small book of verse in his Oxford days, had won for himself the undesirable appellation of 'the clever Marden'; his wife, who survived him three years, had a reputation for gaiety and skirt-dancing which fitted ill the Marden manner; and nobody, least of all Aunt Julia, could doubt that Providence, which saw best in these matters, never really intended either of them to reign at Marden House. In due time, then, George succeeded: owner of Heaven knows how many acres, and guardian of the plumpest, bluest-eyed, yellowest-haired four-year-old in the county. This was Dinah.

No doubt there was a time when Dinah held out uncertain hands from her cradle to the rather wistful Roger who pondered her; no doubt she learnt, a year or two later, to distinguish between the gay young woman who showed her off and the gay young women who admired her; but she had no sad memories for her parents. Life was great fun with Uncle George as father. Nor were Aunt Julia's occasional interventions as mother unappreciated. Lady Marden preached one gospel only—Fresh Air and Exercise; and if she strode over from the Warren once a week, simply to interrupt a French lesson with the command, 'Get that girl out more,' how could Dinah not be grateful? Later, perhaps, Aunt Julia would not be so welcome, but by that time there was to be a new mother—the adorable Olivia.

In the early days George and Dinah were great friends. George was her king; he could do no wrong. All that she wanted, when they took their walks together—she skipping by his side, leaving him for a solitary adventure and then hurrying back to his comforting hand, making with much laughter from both of them her short fat legs do the stride of his—all that she wanted was facts. Why did this do that, who made the little pigs, what were trees for? George gave her facts, such facts as seemed good for her, and if sometimes his opinions crept into them—as when she asked him why Lumsden didn't live in a big house, too—they were accepted as facts just as confidently. Uncle George knew everything and *he* didn't tell little girls not to ask questions.

But that blessed age (to Authority) when one is accepted as all-wise cannot go on for ever. By the time when Olivia came to Marden House, Dinah was not so sure of George, nor George of Dinah. They were still great friends, but George was no longer king. Besides, there was a queen now. It was Olivia and Dinah who had the 'lovely times' together; possibly Olivia and George, too—Dinah did not bother her head about that; but the George-Dinah affair was over.

'And to think,' said Dinah to Brian, 'that there was once a time when I thought he knew everything!'

'I don't want to say anything against your uncle—'

'I do,' said Dinah frankly.

'But there are moments when he seems to me—correct me if I'm wrong—a trifle lacking in enthusiasm about my pictures.'

'Y-yes. I think that is so.'

'And there is also something about my personality which fails to fascinate him. Is it not so?'

'It is,' gurgled Dinah.

'It's very odd. You know, when I first came here, I thought I was having a success with George. I said to myself, "I've got this man George in my pocket. I can do anything with him." But I was wrong.'

'I'm afraid you were, darling.'

They were silent for a little. Dinah was thinking that, after all, it *was* rather fun being forbidden by a stern guardian to marry the man you loved. Because it made it all rather exciting, and it wasn't as if he could really *do* anything. She was nineteen.

What can you do to nineteen when it defies you? She smiled to herself as she thought what fun it was.

'Do you mind not doing that?' said Brian.

'Not doing what?'

'Looking so adorable … No, now you're doing it again. Stop it! Remember what George said: "No love-making."'

Dinah laughed and jumped up.

'Come on. Let's go back and see what's happened.'

'Do you think there's any chance?' said Brian, getting up slowly. 'You know, I doubt, if even Olivia could persuade George to love me in twenty minutes.'

'You don't know Olivia. She's wonderful.'

'Well, if she can do that, I shall take off my hat to her.'

They found Olivia in the morning-room, busy with the curtains.

'Finished?' asked Dinah, as they came in.

'Oh, no, I've got all these rings to put on.'

'I meant talking to George.'

'We walked about outside,' said Brian proudly, 'and we didn't kiss each other once.'

But, of course, Olivia didn't understand what an amazing amount of self-control this implied.

'Brian was very George-like,' complained Dinah. 'He wouldn't even let me tickle the back of his neck.' She realized suddenly that this was not a very pretty thing to say to George's wife, and she flung her arms round Olivia's neck, and added hastily, 'Darling, being George-like is a very *nice* thing to be—' No, that wasn't quite right somehow—'I mean a very nice thing for other people to be—'. Nor was that. She tried again. 'I mean—oh, well, you know what I mean. But do say he's going to be decent about it.'

'Of course he is, Dinah.'

'You mean,' said Brian eagerly, 'he'll let me come here as—as—'

'As my young man?'

'Oh, I think so,' said Olivia.

'Brian!' She flung herself at him, and then broke away to clasp Olivia. 'Olivia, you're a wonder! Have you really talked him round?'

'Well, I haven't said anything yet.'

'O Lord!' groaned Brian.

'But I dare say I shall think of something.' Dinah's mouth dropped. Her eyes were tragic.

'After all, Dinah,' said her lover bravely, 'I'm going back to London to-morrow, anyhow, so—'

'You can be good for one more day,' Olivia comforted her, 'and then when Brian isn't here, we'll see what we can do.'

'I'm more lovable when I'm away,' explained Brian.

'Yes, but I didn't want him to go back to-morrow.'

'Must,' said Brian sternly. 'Hard work before me.' He expanded himself. 'Paint the Mayor and Corporation of Pudsey, life-size, including chains of office. Paint slice of lemon on plate. Copy Landseer for old gentleman in Bayswater. Design antimacassars for middle-aged sofa in Streatham. Earn thousands a year for you, Dinah.'

She broke into her sudden surprising laugh, and all was summer again.

'Oh, Brian, you're heavenly! What fun we shall have when we're married!'

'Sir Brian Strange, R.A., if you please,' he corrected her with dignity. He lay back in a chair and gazed into the future. 'Sir Brian Strange, R.A., writes, "Your Sanogene has proved a most excellent tonic. After completing the third acre of my academy picture, 'The Mayor and Corporation of Pudsey,' I was completely exhausted. But one bottle of Sanogene revived me, and I finished the remaining seven acres at a single sitting."'

Olivia smiled and looked into her work-basket, where her scissors always should be but never were.

'Brian, find my scissors for me.'

'Scissors!' said Brian pompously. 'Sir Brian Strange, R.A., looks for scissors.' He hobbled round the room as well as the gouty leg of Sir Brian would let him, and looked for scissors. Lady Strange, also rather gouty, hobbled after him. 'Scissors ... scissors ... Aha!' He wheeled round dramatically upon Lady Strange and brandished the scissors.

'Once more we must record an unqualified success for the eminent academician.' He bowed low to the laughing Olivia. 'Your scissors, madam.'

'Thank you so much,' she said, looking at him fondly, and hoping that he might ever keep as young.

'Come on, Brian, let's go out,' said the now quite happy Dinah. 'I feel open-airy.'

'Don't be late for lunch, there's good peoples. Lady Marden is coming.'

'Aunt Juli-ah! Help!' cried Dinah and fainted in Brian's arms. 'That means a clean pinafore,' she said, on recovering. 'Brian, you'll jolly well have to brush your hair.'

He felt it a little anxiously.

'I wonder if there would be time to go up to London and get it cut,' he murmured.

But before he was able to do anything about it Anne was at the door.

'Mr. Pim,' she announced.

II

Mr. Pim's telegram, phrased as courteously as might be for the money, told his sister Prudence that he would be with her on the morrow in time for lunch. His letter had added that he was bringing her some fresh flowers from the country, but such an announcement could hardly bear the emphasis of the telegraphed word, so that the flowers would now be a surprise to her. It was Brymer's idea, naturally—the flowers being his in the first place—and he would explain this to her when he saw her. Prudence was very fond of flowers; she felt that they made the house look cheerful.

He came out from the cool shade of the post office (or grocer's, if you were buying groceries), and blinked for a moment in the sunlight, wondering where he was going next. Brymer, coming round the corner quickly, pulled Polly up in time, and hailed him.

'Hallo! Well met. I'll drive you to the Trevors. Save you a walk.'

'Thank you, thank you,' said Mr. Pim, preparing to climb up. 'Whoa, Polly! ... Can you manage it?'

'I think so, thank you.'

'Allow me, sir,' said the grocer's young man, hurrying out.

'Please don't trouble,' said Mr. Pim, and was explaining that he had done it before, indeed only that morning, when a heave from the grocer's young man, and a hand from Brymer, left him a trifle breathless in his place, and Polly was off again.

'Thank you, thank you,' said Mr. Pim, and raised his hat to the grocer's young man, who grinned, 'Not at all, sir,' and went back to his biscuits.

'George give you that letter all right?' said Brymer.

The world was going a little too quickly for Mr. Pim. George? George? He put his hand in his pocket and pulled out his letter to Prudence. Yes, that was the letter which he ought to have posted yesterday. But he had seen about that. He had just sent a telegram.

'Roger knew Fanshawe well. He was the clever one, you know ... Steady, old girl.'

Mr. Pim realized where he was suddenly.

'I am going back now to get the letter,' he explained. 'Mr. Marden was out when I called, so I just sent off an important telegram, and now I am going back.'

'Whoa, Polly!' Brymer pulled up. 'You want to go back to George's?'

'Please, yes.'

Brymer gave a little laugh, half of annoyance, half of amusement. 'Well, we're going the wrong way,' he said. And he turned the mare round. 'Come on, Polly.'

So in a little while Mr. Pim was giving his name again (quite unnecessarily) to Anne, and for the second time that day was shown into the morning-room of Marden House.

'Mr. Pim!' said Dinah eagerly, seizing his hand. 'Here we are again! You can't get rid of us so easily as you think.'

'My dear Miss Marden, I have no wish—I have just been into the village to send a telegram—'

'How do you do, Mr. Pim?' said Olivia, coming with a smile to his rescue. 'Do sit down, won't you? My husband will be here directly. Anne, send somebody down to the farm—'

'I think I heard Mr. Marden in the library, madam.'

'Oh, then tell him, will you?'

'Yes, madam,' said Anne, and went out.

Mr. Pim sat down nervously on the sofa next to Olivia. What was it that the girl had been telling him about her? Something about Australia, wasn't it, or was he thinking of somebody else? How interesting if she knew Australia, too!

'You'll stay to lunch, of course, Mr. Pim?'

'Oh, do!' put in Dinah eagerly, and Brian also smiled at him in an encouraging way, feeling that his presence at lunch would ease Lady Marden a little.

'It's very kind of you, Mrs. Marden, but—'

'Oh, you simply must, Mr. Pim,' said the ridiculous Dinah. 'You haven't told us half enough about yourself yet. I want to know all about your early life, and where you went to school, and if you were—'

'Dinah!' This from Olivia, shaking her head at her niece, and pretending to be shocked.

'Oh, but we are almost, I might say, old friends, Mrs. Marden,' explained Mr. Pim. How young, how fresh, the girl was! But also how alarming.

'Of course we are! There's more in Mr. Pim than you think. He knows Brian, too. Brian, did you say "How do you do?" again?' Brian grinned. 'That's right. You *will* stay to lunch, won't you?'

Mr. Pim turned to Olivia.

'It's very kind of you to ask me, Mrs. Marden,' he said, 'but I am afraid I am lunching with the Trevors.'

'Oh, well, you must come to lunch another day.'

'Thank you, thank you.' Should he explain that he was going back to London on the morrow? Perhaps no. After all, he would be in this part of the country again some day.

Meanwhile Dinah was chattering on.

'The reason why we like Mr. Pim so much is that he was the first person to congratulate us. We feel that he is going to have a great influence on our young lives. What is it, Brian?' She turned severely to her young friend, who looked very grave suddenly and said that it was nothing.

Mr. Pim explained courteously to Olivia.

'I—er—so to speak, stumbled upon the engagement this morning, and—er—I ventured—'

'Oh, yes. Children, you must go and tidy yourselves up. Run along.'

Brian explained with great dignity that Sir Brian and Lady Strange never ran; they walked. With a graceful bow he offered his arm to her ladyship. She curtsied deeply. Then, as they passed Mr. Pim, she threw him a condescending *'Au revoir!'*

He got up, chuckling.

'Good morning, Miss Marden.'

Dinah bent her head, and with a hand to her mouth whispered dramatically, 'We—shall—meet—*again*!' And so out of the room on Brian's arm to the changing of that pinafore.

Mr. Pim loved it. He chuckled and nodded his head. 'What youth, what youth!' his eyes said through his spectacles to the loving, indulgent eyes of Olivia.

'You must forgive them,' said Olivia. 'They are such children. And you can understand that they are a little excited just now.'

'But, of course, Mrs. Marden, of course.'

'Naturally,' she went on casually, 'you won't say anything about their engagement. We only heard about it ourselves five minutes ago, and of course nothing has been settled yet.'

Out of the corner of her eye she looked at him a little anxiously. Suppose some of the Trevors turned up at tea-time with congratulations! Poor George! She smiled a little at the idea, but it would be very awkward. Fortunately, Mr. Pim reassured her that he would not dream of saying anything to anybody.

'Thank you, Mr. Pim.' The door opened. 'Ah, here is my husband. George, this is Mr. Pim.'

George held out his hand with a smile of welcome.

Chapter Seven

A Voice from the Past

I

The little pigs had called to George, but he did not hear them. Important business with Lumsden called him, the estate clamoured for him, but he did not answer. He sat in the library, pretending to read the paper; he stood up and filled his pipe; he lit it and let it go out; he strode up and down the room, lit his pipe again, sat down, stood up, looked out of the window, and came back once more to his chair.

'That must be regarded as my last word on the subject.'

But was it?

He went over and over in his mind all that he had said. And thrice he routed all his foes and thrice he slew the slain ... but Olivia's face, calm, undisturbed, was still before him. What would she do?

Just suppose for a moment—never mind this stupid boy and girl engagement business—just suppose for a moment that Olivia put those curtains up. Impossible, of course; he had definitely forbidden it; but just suppose. What would he do? Give orders to Anne that they should be taken down again? Then all the servants would know that he and she had quarrelled, and that she had disobeyed him. Impossible! Leave them up, then? Impossible, too. That would be the end of everything. But what could he *do*?

Poor George! He was realizing for the first time that, once you begin to ask yourself what is the basis of moral authority, you find that it has none. 'I forbid you to do that,' says husband to wife. So long as the wife concedes him the authority, all is well. But should she question it, his power is gone. 'I forbid you to do that' means no more than 'I shall be very much annoyed if you do that.' To which the answer may be, 'Well, I shall be very much annoyed if I don't.' The wife, in fact, can say 'I forbid' to her husband with no less meaning and no less authority. The penalty in either case is a frown and a cold cheek. Which of them minds it more?

Poor George! He liked to be comfortable. All his life there had been a conspiracy among the gods to make him comfortable. They had got him born in Marden House; they had removed Roger at the right moment; they had sent him Olivia. Olivia had made him very comfortable. That, thought George, was the woman's mission in life. The woman made things easy for the man, so that he could devote his great mind undisturbed to the business of earning a living for them both, or, in some cases, looking after the living which other people earned for them. But how could he be comfortable if Olivia turned against him? If she flouted his orders, and encouraged Dinah to rebel? Even if she obeyed, with a frown and a cold cheek, would he be comfortable then?

But, of course, it was ridiculous to think such uncomfortable things. Olivia was Olivia, the woman he loved, the perfect wife. She had been foolish to-day; well, these last few days; not herself. The weather, perhaps, had been a trifle too hot—one must make allowances. And she was right about those curtains; it would be stupid to waste the material. He would suggest that they should be put up in Dinah's bedroom. Dinah would like it, and Olivia would feel that her curtains had not been wasted. And then, as soon as that damned fellow Strange was out of the house, they could all be happy again.

But now another uncomfortable thought came creeping into his mind. Telworthy a convict! This was the first he had heard of it; well, the first time he had had to listen to it. A Marden had married the widow of a convict!

Until that morning Telworthy had been little more than an unfortunate. Luck had been against him; he had had to go to Australia—like many another younger son. Very conveniently he had died in Australia. Since he was dead, there was no need to think about him. George never thought about him. But now—a convict! Damn the fellow! Why couldn't he have been more careful?

'So, you see, we need not be too particular about our niece.'

What on earth possessed Olivia to make her talk like that? What had Telworthy got to do with it? Olivia was a Marden now; Dinah had always been a Marden. What did it matter what Telworthy had done? Olivia was a Marden now—his wife. There was no tarnish on the Marden name. Why should Dinah marry any Tom, Dick or Harry who came along, just because Olivia— but there was no need to think about that; the fellow was dead.

'Mr. Pim, sir; he is in the morning-room.'

George came out of his thoughts with a start. 'Who? Oh, of course, Mr. Pim. Thank you.' He wanted a letter. Ask him to stay to lunch. Aunt Julia was coming, too. Make things easier. By to-morrow, when that fellow Strange had gone, they would all be comfortable again ... And—yes—the curtains should go up in Dinah's room. Then they would *all* be happy.

II

'Well, Mr. Pim, we meet at last. Sorry to have kept you waiting before.'

'The apology should come from me, Mr. Marden, for having trespassed in this way on your good nature.'

'Not at all,' said George, with his pleasant smile. 'Any friend of Brymer's—'

Olivia looked at her husband, and thought what a nice, good, clean, handsome husband he was. She always liked him thus, the Englishman in his castle, welcoming the stranger by the way. There was an air about him. She felt that Mr. Pim felt it; that he was impressed by George's ease, his sureness, even his physical well-being. What matter if George had no right to be so sure? The effect was the same. She felt suddenly that it was fun having disagreements with him, because there he was always, her husband who loved her, whom she loved (nothing could alter that), and they had the joy of making it up again. If you never went away, you never had the pleasure of coming back.

'Let's see, you want a letter to this man Fanshawe?' said George, sitting down at his desk.

'Shall I be in the way?' asked Olivia, half getting up.

'Oh no, no, please don't,' said Mr. Pim.

'It's only a question of a letter, dear.' He saw the curtains again, but he did not frown now. They were going up in Dinah's room. She was quite right to get on with them.

'Fanshawe will put you in the way of seeing all that you want to see,' went on George. 'My brother Roger and he were great friends.'

He began to write, but looked up to say, 'You'll stay to lunch, of course?'

'It is very kind of you, but I am lunching with the Trevors.'

George was disappointed. Fortunately there was still Aunt Julia.

'Ah, well, they'll look after you all right. Good chap, Trevor.'

'Yes, yes, undoubtedly.' He turned politely to Olivia. 'You see, Mrs. Marden,' he explained, 'I have only recently arrived from Australia, after travelling about the world for some years, and I am a little out of touch with my fellow-workers in London.'

Olivia was interested. 'So you've been in Australia, Mr. Pim?' she said.

George did not like it. Surely, after what had come out this morning, the less that was said about Australia the better. Olivia ought to have had more tact. He cleared his throat loudly in a way which would indicate to her the need for tact, and assured Mr. Pim that he would soon have the letter ready for him.

'Thank you, thank you,' said Mr. Pim, with a little bow. 'Oh yes, Mrs. Marden, I have been in Australia more than once in the last few years.'

'Really?' She took a mischievous glance at George's back, and went on: 'I used to live at Sydney many years ago. Do you know Sydney at all?'

George cleared his throat in a manner still more threatening. He turned round to them, pen in hand—officially in order to suggest to Mr. Pim some small point in connexion with the letter he was writing, but unofficially to frown at his wife for her continued tactlessness.

'Indeed, yes,' said Mr. Pim. 'I have often stayed at Sydney. On the last occasion for several months.'

'Fancy! I wonder if we have any friends in common there?'

This was terrible. In another moment all Telworthy's shady history would be dragged into the light.

'Extremely unlikely,' said George gruffly. 'Sydney is a very big place.'

'True,' said Mr. Pim, in his gentle reproachful voice, 'but the world is a very small place, Mr. Marden.' He gazed up at the ceiling, and went on dreamily. 'I had a remarkable instance of that coming over in the boat on this last occasion.'

'Ah!' said George, with a sigh of relief. The conversation was safe now; let the old gentleman babble on. Some dull story of some dull coincidence interesting as a happening at first-hand, but as a story at second-hand, always wearisome; he knew the sort. But safe, safe. With a smile for the old gentleman he went back to his letter.

'Most remarkable instance,' meditated Mr. Pim. 'A man I used to know in Sydney—'

He told his little story, Olivia listening with her encouraging smile. About a man who had been in prison in Sydney—fraudulent company-promoting or something of the sort—and when he came out Mr. Pim gave him employment, but he was a bad character, Mrs. Marden, a bad character. Poor fellow! He took to drink, and was drinking himself into his grave; Mr. Pim gave him another month to live. All this had happened years ago, and yet, oddly enough (showing what a small place the world is), the very first person whom Mr. Pim saw as he stepped on to the boat which had just brought him from Australia was this same poor fellow!

'Fancy!' said Olivia. What else could you say to a dull story like that? But she said it just as if it had been the best story which she had heard that year.

'Oh, yes,' said Mr. Pim, nodding his head emphatically. 'There was no mistaking him. I spoke to him, in fact; we recognized each other.'

'Fancy!' said Olivia again.

'Yes indeed! As it happened, he was travelling steerage, and we did not come across each other once we were at sea; and unfortunately at Marseilles this poor fellow—' He broke off and gazed up at the ceiling. 'Now what *was* his name?'

George addressed his letter, and got up from his desk with a smile. A dull story.

'It was a very unusual one,' said Mr. Pim, still struggling with his memories. 'A very unusual one. It began with a—with a T, I think.'

Fear, wild unreasoning fear, leapt suddenly into Olivia's eyes, and flashed its message across to her husband. 'George, say something! Say it's impossible ... Oh, quick, quick! I'm frightened, dear, I'm frightened. Help me, my husband.'

He was by her side at once. He was holding her hand. 'Nonsense, dear, nonsense,' he was saying. He was stroking her hand.

'Quick, Mr. Pim, quick!'

A quiet satisfaction spread itself over Mr. Pim's face. What a memory he had for his age! He never forgot a name—never!

'I've got it!' he said, beaming at them. 'Telworthy.' He leant back proudly.

'Telworthy!' Olivia whispered to herself. She gave a little shudder.

'Good God!' cried George.

Pleased with the success of his story Mr. Pim nodded at them.

'Telworthy. An unusual name, is it not? Certainly not a name which you could forget when once you had heard it.'

'No,' said Olivia, in a slow dead voice, 'it is not a name which you can forget when once you have heard it.'

III

Olivia sat looking into the past. There rose before her the evening when she first discovered what it was she had married.

Her amazed protest.

'But it's not honest!'

'D'you mean it's illegal?'

'Naturally, I don't know anything about the law, but —'

'Well, it happens that I do, my dear. You may take it from me that it can be done quite safely ... D'you mind if I smoke?'

He lit his cigar.

'But, Jacob?'

His amused smile.

'Well, Livvy?'

'It isn't honest.'

'It's business, my dear.'

'Aren't men ever honest in business?'

'Men aren't such fools as to take it for granted that the other fellow will be what you call honest. They know what the law allows him to do, and they take their precautions. That's business.'

'How horrible!'

His patronizing smile.

'Well, I didn't ask *you* to come into it, did I, Livvy? You look after the house—that's your job. I'll look after the money—that's my job.'

'But it's other people's money. They trust you.' His amused smile.

'And my wife doesn't.'

His amused laugh when she had stood up, saying nothing. His careless kiss on her cheek as he went past her to open the door. His closing of the door as she came up to it, his steady survey of her from head to foot, and his final easy pronouncement before he let her go:

'You know, Livvy, you're much too pretty to bother your head about money. Leave it to the ugly devils like me.'

That other evening.

He had come into her bedroom. She was sitting in front of her glass, and he stood behind her, looking at her reflection with that amused smile of his. Then, in admiration:

'Damn it, Livvy, but you're a beauty.'

'Is that what you came in to tell me?'

'Well, no!' He laughed. Then, after a pause, 'How long does it take you to pack?'

'To pack?' She hadn't understood.

'Yes. Ten minutes—or a week? I'm afraid a week's too long.'

'But to go where?'

'Australia.'

'Australia? Why?'

'Well, the fact is, we've made the Old Country a bit too hot for us.'

'We!'

'Telworthy,' he explained easily. 'Your name, too, my dear.'

They were still looking at each other in the glass. Now she turned round to him.

'You mean that if we stay in England—'

'I go to prison. Yes. Pleasant country, England. Delightful county, Devonshire. Dartmoor, picturesque spot, they tell me.'

His amused smile again. How she hated it! If he had only been frightened!

'I knew it would happen.'

'Oh, come, Livvy! That isn't worthy of you.'

'"You may take it from me that it can be done quite safely!" It was the one thing you boasted about.'

'Yes, but this was something extra. I took the risk and—we're going to Australia.'

'Don't they have prisons there?'

'We shall discover the habits of the native when we arrive. We sail the day after to-morrow. Can you be ready?'

She had been frightened then.

'To-morrow, Jacob, to-morrow! It might be too late after-wards.'

His easy laugh.

'Don't be alarmed, my dear. He has given us until the end of the week.'

'Who?'

'The gentleman whose signature I borrowed.'

'Forgery!'

'The last throw of the defeated general. We retreat in good order to Australia. Happy, happy country, in which all the men are good, and all the women beautiful. But none so beautiful as my Livvy.'

And he had come to life again!

IV

'Telworthy! Good God!' That, and no more, was the burden of George Marden's thoughts as he hurried Mr. Pim out of the house, down the drive, out of the gates. 'Telworthy! Good God!' he was still saying to himself as he hurried back to Olivia. If once he stopped saying that, he would have to think and he did not dare to think. Thinking would hurt. His mind was numbed by one overpowering confused sense of outrage; he shrank from the pain of its returning struggle to consciousness. 'Telworthy! Good God!'

You may shout a toothache down for twenty seconds, perhaps for a minute, but it wins in the end. George could not control his brain for long. Before he was half-way back to Olivia it had got to work again. And the first thing it asked him, asked him with amazement, was how he could have thought himself ill-used before, how he could have complained that his day was going badly, quarrelled with Olivia, wrangled with Brian; how he could have failed to realize, and to thank Heaven for it, that he was the happiest, the luckiest, the most-to-be-envied man in all the county of Buckinghamshire—or in all the countries of the world for that matter—before Mr. Pim came. You fool, George; you blind fool!

Oh, to be back where he was ten minutes ago! What ridiculously trivial things quarrels about curtains were, and engagements of nieces! How little they mattered. Ten minutes ago he and Olivia lived happily together in this dear comfortable house of his—look at its warm red bricks, its mullioned windows, its tall square chimneys—and now ... Oh, to be back where he was! Never, never, never would he complain again. But no, it was too late. Telworthy had come to life. Telworthy! ... Good God!

Meanwhile, Mr. Pim, happy in the success of his little anecdote about the man from Sydney, was making his benign way to the Trevors. As Mr. Marden had said, a good fellow, Trevor.

Chapter Eight

Aunt Julia

I

Lady Marden—'Aunt Juli-ah, help!' as Dinah invariably called her—widow of that famous statesman, Sir John Marden, was a weather-beaten woman in the sixties. No doubt the weather of the British Isles is detestable at times, but Lady Marden always seemed to have been out in the worst of it. It may be that when, as commonly reported in the papers, a cyclone was 'approaching from the North-West of Ireland,' Lady Marden travelled with it, thus benefiting all the way from its rigours. Even were she shown into your drawing-room on a hot August afternoon, you would say to yourself, 'How damnable it must be outside,' and order the fire to be lit. 'If she had been whaling for sixty years in the Arctic,' said Dinah bitterly, 'she couldn't look more like it than she does.'

She had done her duty by the late President of the Local Government Board as wife and mother. Three daughters she had given him, in spite of the inevitable interference on each occasion with the hunting season, and those three girls she had brought up on the best principles of fresh air, cold water, and exercise. 'Look at Marion!' she would say to George, when urging upon him, in his niece's presence, a more Spartan method with Dinah, and Dinah would say unkindly, 'Well, look at her!'

Marion Marden, Muriel Marden and Matilda Marden were the names which she had given to her three lean greyhounds from the Marden stock; good fellows all, but Dinah had no wish to compete with them.

George's marriage was a great disappointment to his Aunt Julia. It was essential that he should bring home a wife some day, pleasant though it was meanwhile to mother—if you can call it mothering—the girl for him, and order about his servants, but Olivia was not the wife she would have chosen. A widow of no family!—such as might be expected, perhaps, to excite the callow affections of a boy fresh from school, but to win the love of a healthy, well-exercised, well-tubbed man of affairs like George, never! However, he was the head of the house; it was not her business to interfere. She knew George; she knew him well enough to feel that, whatever Olivia might have been in the past, he would see to it that from the day of their marriage she would be nothing more nor less than Marden.

Aunt Julia lunched at Marden House once a week. This being so, there should have been six days a week, three hundred and twelve in the year, when Aunt Julia did not lunch at Marden House. To Dinah it hardly seemed so many. If she had to wait until she was twenty-one before she could marry Brian, the intervening two years would appear ridiculously short reckoned as only a hundred and four more lunches for Aunt Julia. Why, that was nothing; Aunt-Julia-help would work that off in no time. The weeks flashed into a succession of milestones engraved 'Lady Marden.'

She could make this claim as guest, that she presented no terrors to the housewife. Cold beef and pickles, my dear George, with a tankard of ale and a good ripe cheese was enough for any man or woman. Cold beef it was, whenever she came to lunch, and Olivia and Dinah could peck away at French fal-lals if they pleased. But not entirely without comment. Her duty to her country impelled Aunt Julia to point out once a week that the Spanish Armada (to take a case) had been defeated by British beef and beer, and she still seemed to hope that, at the last moment, one or other of the weaklings might swerve aside from the *ragoût* out of respect for those early heroes. In vain. They only passed her the mustard ...

But why did she choose to-day, of all days, to come to lunch? 'Excellent beef this, George.'

'What?' He came back to her with a start. 'Oh yes, yes, excellent.' He returned to his thoughts again.

Dinah looked at her uncle wonderingly, and then to Olivia at the other end of the table, asking for information. But Olivia was in the same case. Her thoughts were as far away as George's. What had happened? It was no simple quarrel about herself, her engagement to Brian. This was not George's manner when he was being the determined head of the house who had said his last word on the subject. 'No, I believe it's Mr. Pim,' said Dinah to herself.

'You ought to try a slice of this beef, Olivia.'

'Beef?' said Olivia vaguely. 'Oh, no thank you, Aunt Julia.' She looked across at Dinah. Was it an appeal for help, for relief from interruption of her thoughts? Dinah took it as that; and, with a warning pressure of Brian's foot, and a twinkle at him when he looked round inquiringly, she plunged in.

'I'm giving up beef, Aunt Julia,' she said. 'I've decided to be a vegetarian.'

'Vegetarian? Rubbish! What's the matter with the girl?'

'Nothing's the matter with me, but I think it's so cruel.'

'Cruel! God bless us!' She turned to her nephew. 'George, what's this nonsense?'

'Uncle George doesn't know yet. It has been coming over me for some weeks, but I haven't said anything to anybody. I want to talk quietly to a clergyman first. Anne, some more beans, please.'

Lady Marden looked at her with her hard bright eyes and snorted.

'You've been reading some Radical rubbish in a book. Cruel! Why, bless the girl, what d'you suppose God put animals into the world *for*?'

'To sing to us,' said Dinah gently.

Brian dived hastily under the table for his napkin ...

And there she sat, Olivia, his wife, but his wife no longer. What was Dinah talking about? 'Of course not, Aunt Julia, of course not.' What was it she said? ... Telworthy alive— then Olivia had never been his wife at all. How beautiful she was. But not his wife—Telworthy's. What an *awful* thing to have happened! What were they going to do? What *could* they do? What an endless meal it was ... 'No thank you.' They must talk it over after lunch together, after this endless meal. 'Oh, I beg your pardon, Aunt Julia.' Good God, she wanted some more.

'And you'd better give yourself some, George, and keep me company.'

Well, perhaps he had. It was something to do ... Oh, eat, Aunt Julia, eat, don't waste time talking. Dinah, hold your tongue, you're interrupting her ... Oh, Olivia! Get rid of them somehow, and talk to me.

Olivia looked across at her husband, read the torment in his face, and gave a little reassuring smile. Poor George! How hateful it was going to be for him. And it was just her mischief in talking to Mr. Pim about Australia which had brought it all about. Even if Telworthy had stayed in England, he would never have found out; they would never have met again. Even if Mr. Pim had told his anecdote at the Trevors' or the Brymers', nobody would have associated a drunken convict with her first husband. She had brought it on them herself; it was her own fault. 'Oh, George, I *am* so sorry.'

Brian and Dinah were at the gooseberry-tart stage.

'I wonder you don't think it cruel eating the poor goose-berries, Dinah,' said Lady Marden sarcastically.

'Oh, it isn't cruel eating gooseberries,' explained Dinah. 'It's very cruel eating raspberries and blackberries, because they've always got little animals on them, but gooseberries are quite safe. I'm giving up blackberries altogether.' She turned to Brian. 'I hope you will too, Mr. Strange. You would never forgive yourself if you bit into a honeymoon suddenly. They may be small, but they feel it just as deeply as we do.' She paused, and then added thoughtfully: 'None of my gooseberries have shaved for a long time.'

Poor George! How hateful it was going to be for him. What would happen? They would have to get married again or something. How silly the law was. What was going on inside George's head? Handsome George, clean, handsome George … let me put my arms round you, dear, and comfort you. It's nothing to worry about. He will go back to Australia; he will want to go back. England isn't safe for him. Oh, George, George, he's a horrible man—you don't know him—I've never told you. But he will go back. You will send him back.

'Excellent Stilton this, George.'

'What? … Oh, yes, yes, Aunt Julia. Glad you like it. Have some more, won't you?'

'No, thanks.'

Thank God!

'Some cheese, Mr. Strange?' said Dinah.

Dinah, don't be a confounded little idiot. If that fellow Strange has any cheese, I'll *never* let him marry Dinah—never, never, never, if he lives to be a hundred.

Brian's fate is in the balance. Will he get George's consent when he is ninety-nine?

He will.

'No cheese, thank you, Miss Marden.'

Saved!

'Shall we have coffee outside, Aunt Julia?'

Oh, bless you, Olivia! To be outside where one can think properly! And we'll send Aunt Julia off to look at the pigs, and then —

'Thank you, Olivia. If I had my way, I'd have every meal outside, only the servants don't like it.'

She is wiping her mouth. Another minute now and we shall be out.

'Well, that's what I call a sensible lunch.'

She is getting up. Lunch is over. Thank God, it's over. There is still coffee to be got through, but now we can smoke a pipe and think it out properly.

But—what the devil are we going to *do*?

II

Brian saw Dinah only, heard only Dinah. To him this lunch was no different from other lunches at which he and Dinah had sat side by side; or different only in this, that now he could slide his hand underneath the table and be sure of meeting, of saying, 'How do you do?' and 'Good-bye, I must be going now,' to a warm friendly little hand which was always ready for him.

On the terrace, hands were not easy to hold. Wasn't it about time that they got away from all these other people? He caught Dinah's eye, answered her nod, and stood up.

'Oh, Lord, I've forgotten my cigarettes,' he murmured, and drifted back into the house. Presently Dinah joined him.

'Good girl!' He smiled at her.

'Have you found them?' she asked loudly.

'Found what?'

'That was for *their* benefit.' She indicated the terrace. 'I said I'd help you find them. It is your cigarettes we are looking for, isn't it?'

'Yes.' He grinned, and took out his case. 'Have one?'

'No thanks, darling. Aunt Julia still thinks it's unladylike.'

'She would.'

'Have you ever seen her beagling?'

'No. Is that very ladylike?'

'Very. You ought to see her.'

'I shall look forward to it immensely. Any great-aunt of yours beagling—'

'We'll get her to bring the beagles to tea with us in Chelsea one day,' said Dinah carelessly.

To tea with us in Chelsea! Brian looked at her with all his heart in his eyes. Oh, happy, happy days to come!

Dinah interrupted his reverie.

'I say, Brian, what *has* happened, do you think?'

'Everything,' said Brian with conviction. 'I love you, and you love me.'

'Silly! I mean between George and Olivia. Didn't you notice it at lunch?'

'I noticed that you seemed to be doing most of the talking, but then I've noticed that before sometimes. I say, did you hear me agreeing with Lady Marden that Landseer was one of the world's greatest painters? I thought that might do me a bit of good with your uncle.' He expanded his chest proudly. 'Tact!'

'I asked you,' said Dinah sternly, 'whether you noticed George and Olivia at lunch?'

'Yes. No. I mean I noticed that they were there, but—I say, do you think they have quarrelled because of *us*?'

'Of course not. George may think he has quarrelled, but I'm quite sure Olivia hasn't. She never does. No, I believe that Mr. Pim's at the bottom of it. I suspected that man from the first.'

'Yes, you're quite right,' agreed Brian, nodding his head wisely. 'I remember him now. He's Pimlico Pim, the notorious cracksman.'

'No, no, that's his uncle. No, our Pim is just a messenger of evil. He has brought some terribly sad news about George's investments. Ah me! The old home will have to be sold up.'

'Good,' said Brian callously. 'Then your uncle will be only too glad to find somebody to marry you.'

'Yes, darling, but you must be more dramatic about it than that.'

'All right. I'll be more dramatic.'

Dinah pushed him out of the way so as to give herself a little more room in which to be dramatic, and went on:

'"George," you must say, with tears in your eyes, "George, I cannot pay off the whole of the mortgage for you; I have only two and ninepence—"'

'Two and tenpence,' said Brian, bringing out his money from his trousers-pocket.

'"Two and tenpence. But at least let me take your niece off your hands." And then George will thump you on the back and say, "You're a good fellow, Brian, a damn good fellow," and he'll blow his nose very loudly for fear of breaking down altogether, and say, "Confound this cigar, it won't draw properly."' Brian looked at her with a foolish proprietary smile.

'Dinah, you're a heavenly idiot, and I love you. And you've simply got to marry me, uncles or no uncles.'

She bumped down beside him on the sofa.

'It will have to be "uncles", I'm afraid, because, you see, I'm his ward, and I can be sent to Coventry or Chancery or somewhere beastly if I marry without his consent.' She looked at him regretfully. 'Haven't you got anybody who objects to your marrying *me*?'

'Nobody, thank Heaven. I am alone in the world.'

'Well, that's very disappointing of you. I saw myself fascinating your aged father, at the same time that you were fascinating George. I should have done it much better than you.' She shook her head at him sadly. 'As a George-fascinator you aren't very successful, sweetheart. You lack something. A *je ne sais quoi*.'

Brain pulled at his tie, smoothed his eye-brows, and smiled fatuously at her.

'What am I like as a Dinah-fascinator?' he asked.

'Plus six, darling,' she said promptly.

'Good. Then I'll stick to that, and leave George to Olivia.'

'Oh, I expect she'll manage him all right. I have great faith in Olivia.' She turned to him impetuously. 'But you'll marry me, anyhow, won't you, Brian?'

'I will.'

'Even if we have to wait until I am twenty-one?'

'Even,' said Brian firmly, 'if we have to wait until you are fifty-one.'

'Darling!' she cried, flinging her arms round his neck.

He disengaged himself hastily.

'No, no, don't do that. Please!'

'Why not? What's the good of being engaged if you can't do that?'

'I promised your uncle that I wouldn't kiss you. You mustn't tempt me, Dinah, you really mustn't.'

'Oh! I beg your pardon, Mr. Strange.' She turned her back to him.

'Conceded, Miss Marden.'

'Would it be breaking your word of honour as an English gentleman if you *sent* me a kiss? You can look the other way, as if you didn't know that I was here.'

Brian considered this carefully.

'No, I think I might do that,' he said at last. 'Are you there?'

'Yes!' She got ready to catch it.

'Then look out.' He gave a kiss to the tips of his fingers and flicked it in her direction. She snapped it as it went past, and put it to her lips.

'Oh, well caught!'

'Now then, here's one coming for you.'

It was a high dropping one, but Brian negotiated it safely. He rose and bowed.

'Madam, I thank you.'

She curtsied to him.

'Your servant, sir.'

III

George was in the library writing a note and giving instructions to the waiting servant. At last there was something to be done; why hadn't he thought of it before? It was necessary that they should get hold of Mr. Pim. They must hear from his own lips that fatal word again—Telworthy. You're sure his name was Telworthy, Mr. Pim? Quite sure, Mr. Marden. And you knew him in Sydney, a convict, a fraudulent company-promoter, a drinker? Yes, Mr. Marden, that is so. And he is alive now? Alive now, Mr. Marden ... George rehearsed to himself the conversation which would inevitably take place, yet felt that he must make certain of it. They must see Mr. Pim once more.

'I want one of the men to drive over to the Trevors',' he said as he sealed up the note to Mr. Pim, 'deliver this letter, and then bring Mr. Pim back here. Is that clear?'

'Yes, sir.'

He handed over the letter and went back to the terrace. Lady Marden and Olivia were talking in an uninterested and desultory way, and his aunt shook herself off with a sigh of relief as soon as George appeared.

'Well, are we going down to see the pigs?'

No, that was something that George would *not* do.

'Take Dinah down, won't you, Aunt Julia? There's a little business, I have to discuss with Olivia. I'll join you later.'

'Very well. Where is the girl?'

Where was she? Gone off with that fellow Strange somewhere. This was damnable. 'Dinah!' he called threateningly.

'Hallo!' from the morning-room.

Thank heavens!

Dinah came out, followed by Brian.

'Do you want me?'

'Aunt Julia wants to see the pigs, dear,' said Olivia. 'I wish you would take her down. Your uncle has some business to attend to, and'—she smiled adorably at Dinah—'I'm rather tired.'

'Right-o.'

'I've always said that you don't take enough exercise, Olivia,' put in Lady Marden. 'Look at me!—sixty-five and proud of it.'

Brian looked at her wonderingly.

'Yes, Aunt Julia, you're marvelous,' said Olivia gently.

But Dinah was not going to stand any criticism of her deity.

'How old would Olivia be if she did take exercise?' she asked innocently.

The maddened George broke in.

'Don't stand about asking silly questions, Dinah. Your aunt hasn't too much time.'

Brian asked if he might come, too—the first sensible thing which George had heard him say at Marden House.

'Well, a little exercise wouldn't do *you* any harm, Mr. Strange.' She looked him over with a professional eye. 'You're an artist, ain't you?'

'Well, I try to paint.'

Dinah hastily explained that he had sold a picture last March for—

'Yes, yes, never mind that now,' shouted George.

'Unhealthy fife,' was Lady Marden's comment on the profession. She strode down the steps of the terrace, throwing the invitation 'Well, come along!' over her shoulder at them. They came along.

'At last!' said George.

'Poor George!' said Olivia tenderly. She gave a little reassuring pat to his arm, and walked into the morning-room. He followed her ...

But what were they going to do?

Chapter Nine

A Good Man's Conscience

What undramatic lives we lead, most of us. We get up, we eat, we work, we play, we go to bed, and in the morning we get up again. Sometimes we are not very well, sometimes we are not very lucky. We make more money to-day than yesterday, or yesterday than to-day; we are annoyed, amused, flattered, offended, happy, unhappy. That is all. We experience how few of the big emotions, how few of the big events. We do not even die until it is too late to be aware of it.

We do well enough without the big emotions. The big emotions are generally uncomfortable, and it is fitting that they should be reserved for others. For we cannot get rid of the idea that there is a Special Providence looking after us, a Providence much more interested, much more careful, than the one which is looking after our neighbour. Others may be run over as they cross the crowded street; that would not surprise us. But it is incredible that it could happen to ourselves. Our first emotion would be not fear, but amazement. Surely a mistake has been made!

So George felt. The thing was unbelievable. He, George Marden, had lived for five years with a woman who was not his wife. It was absurd; it was unreal; it was some fantastic dream for which he had no adequate mental equipment. It was the sort of thing which had happened in books, not in real life, or, if in real life, only to the other people. Not to him, not to George Marden.

He looked across at Olivia, who had gone back placidly to her curtains.

'Well?' he said.

'Well?' said Olivia. 'Now we can talk.'

'At last!' And then he broke out indignantly. 'I'm always glad to see Aunt Julia in my house, but I feel that she needn't have chosen to-day of all days to come to lunch.'

Olivia could not help smiling at the unfairness of this.

'It was really Mr. Pim who chose the wrong day,' she said.

He strode up to her and took her by the arm, almost as if he would shake her out of this incredible dream.

'Good heavens, Olivia, is it true?'

'About Jacob Telworthy?'

'You told me that he was dead. You always said that he was dead. Wasn't he dead?'

'Well, I always thought that he was. He was as dead as anybody could be. All the papers said he was dead.'

'The papers!' said George scornfully.

'*The Times* said he was dead,' she added, as if for George that would be the last word on the subject.

'Oh!' he stuttered, almost in apology.

'Apparently even his death was fraudulent.'

Yet if one could not believe *The Times*, what could one believe? No, it was not Olivia's fault that she had been deceived.

'But what are we going to do?—that's the question. My God, it's horrible! You don't seem to understand, Olivia—you've never been married to me at all!'

'It is a little difficult to realize. You see, it doesn't seem to have made any difference to our happiness.'

'No, that's what's so terrible.'

'Terrible?' Olivia looked at him in amazement.

'I mean,' stumbled George, 'I mean—that is—well, of course, we were quite innocent in the matter. But at the same time nothing can get over the fact that we had no—no right to be happy.'

No right to be happy? But—'Would you rather we had been miserable?' she asked.

Perhaps not that. Yet he felt, poor George, that somehow they had done wrong. The fact that their marriage was not a real Church-blessed, Law-blessed, Heaven-blessed marriage should not have been without its effect. There should have been forebodings, a vague feeling of guilt, an uneasiness; inexplicable until the cause came to light. Then the relief with which he could have said 'No wonder!' It would have been absolution in itself.

George had inherited the religious faith of his fathers, and held it no less firmly than he held their lands, their money, and their political convictions. His face to the east, he proclaimed the details of this faith once every Sunday, a faith which he had taken on trust from his elders, which he had not examined, but which, nevertheless, was his true comfort, inspiration and discipline. He believed in discipline, and not only (as is commonly alleged against his class) in discipline for others. He was eager to obey the particular 'Thou shalts' and 'Thou shalt nots,' under whose protection he had placed himself.

To Olivia, who thought more freely than he, his religious views may have seemed narrow, but it was for their narrowness at first that she had loved him. Telworthy's had been so very broad. To mix again with men and women who divided good from evil, and, having divided them (rightly or wrongly, it mattered not), sought to follow the good, this had been happiness enough for Telworthy's widow.

Ah, but she had never been his widow!

'You're his wife, that's what you don't seem to understand,' cried George, trying to beat it into her brain. 'You're Telworthy's wife! You—er—' He hesitated before he made the awful statement. 'Forgive me, my dear, but it's the horrible truth—you committed bigamy when you married me.' He threw up his hands to the amazing Heaven which had allowed such a thing to happen, and cried again, 'Bigamy!'

'It *is* an ugly word, isn't it?' said Olivia sympathetically. Words had never frightened her, but she knew how terrifying they were to men.

George looked at her in astonishment, wondering how she could be so calm. Why, from the way she behaved, Mr. Pim might never—

A sudden wild hope flashed into his brain. He strode across the room and seized her hands.

'Look here, Olivia, old girl,' he pleaded, with a pathetic attempt at a smile, 'the whole thing is nonsense, eh? It isn't your husband at all; it's some other Telworthy whom this fellow met.' He laughed a little unnaturally, to show that he would be the first to appreciate the humour of it. 'Some other shady swindler who turned up on the boat, eh? I mean, this sort of thing doesn't happen to *us*, committing bigamy and all that. Some other fellow.'

She was silent.

'Olivia!' he pleaded. 'Oh, Olivia, say it was some other fellow!'

She shook her head sadly.

'I knew all the shady swindlers in Sydney, George.' She looked into the past again and summed up the five years of her life with Telworthy. 'They came to dinner ...'

His head comes round her bedroom door.

'Full war-paint to-night, Livvy. We've got a visitor.'

'One of the usual visitors?'

'Pooley. Don't think you know him. Be kind to him. He may be useful.'

Half an hour later. 'My dear, this is Mr. Pooley.'

She gives him her hand, the hand that will never be clean again.

'Glad to meet you, Mrs. Telworthy. Heard so much about you.'

The horrible dinner. The visitor, uneasy, ingratiating, vulgarly deferential; her husband, amused as always, enjoying his guest's discomfort, enjoying his wife's aloofness. 'I know he isn't quite our form,' his smile says to her across the table, 'but we can't all be gentlemen.' The horrible dinner.

It ends at last. She rises.

'I'll leave you to your cigars,' she says, meaning 'to your plots.'

The visitor's clumsy haste to be a gentleman and get to the door first. Her husband still smiling ... Then she is out of the room, and they are alone to work out whatever new method of robbing the public seems most promising. And she—she is one of them.

But there were no others called Telworthy. He was himself, incomparable ...

George dropped into a chair, head in hands. No, he had never really hoped. Telworthy, her husband, was alive.

'Well,' he said at last, 'what are we going to do?'

Olivia came back to the present.

'You sent Mr. Pim away so quickly,' she said. 'We had no time to ask him anything. You hurried him away so quickly.'

'He'll be here directly. I've sent him a note. My one idea at the moment was to get him out of the house—to hush things up.'

She shook her head and smiled sadly.

'You can't hush up two husbands.'

'You can't,' groaned George. 'Everybody will know. Everybody.'

'The children, Aunt Julia, they may as well know now as later. Mr. Pim, of course—'

He interrupted to say with dignity that he did not propose to discuss his affairs, his private affairs, with Mr. Pim. He would only ask him one question: 'Are you absolutely certain that this man's name was Telworthy?' That was all. He could ask it without letting Mr. Pim know the reason for the inquiry. Tactfully.

'You couldn't make a mistake about a name like Telworthy,' said Olivia. 'You can't invent a name like that. But he might tell us something about Telworthy's plans.'

'His plans?'

'Yes. Perhaps he's going back to Australia at once. Perhaps he thinks I'm dead, too. Perhaps—oh, there are so many things I want to know.'

George looked at her in astonishment. What did all this matter? Then, realizing that the shock must have upset her balance a little, he went over to her and spoke soothingly.

'Yes, yes, dear, of course, that would be very interesting. Naturally, we should like to know these things. But you do see, dear, that it doesn't make any difference.'

It was now Olivia's turn to be astonished.

'No difference?'

'Well, obviously you're as much his wife if he is in Australia as you are if he is in England.'

She shook her head, slowly and with absolute conviction.

'I am not his wife at all.'

'Olivia,' he protested, almost peevishly, 'surely you understand the position.'

'Jacob Telworthy may be alive, but I am not his wife. I ceased to be his wife when I became yours.'

'You never *were* my wife,' he burst out. 'That is the terrible part of it. Our union—you make me say it, Olivia—has been unhallowed by the Church, unhallowed even by the Law.' He groaned at the thought of it. 'Legally, we have been living in—' No, it was too awful. 'Living in—' He couldn't get the terrible word out. Yet it was true. They had been living in sin for five years!

She looked up at him, surprised, as if she hardly knew what he was talking about. Then back to her curtains again.

'The point is,' he went on, 'how does the Law stand?'

The Law? What had the Law got to do with right and wrong?

'I imagine,' said the unhappy George, 'that Telworthy could get a divorce!' With himself as co-respondent! Oh, that such things could be happening to him! Surely he would wake up soon—out of this terrible nightmare.

'A divorce!' said Olivia eagerly. 'But then we could *really* get married, and we shouldn't be living in—living in—whatever we were living in before.'

She smiled at him happily. She knew that 'in the eyes of the Law' George and she were no longer husband and wife, but like most women she was entirely without respect for the Law. She had given herself to George five years ago, and it was dazzlingly clear to her that nothing that had happened since could have any effect upon that. Right, Wrong, Law, Church, simply had nothing to do with it. But she understood George's sensitiveness to the opinions of his neighbours. If George's Law and Church, which was another way of saying George's neighbours, maintained that he and Olivia were not husband and wife, George would be unhappy. A divorce from Telworthy, a re-marriage to George, would make him happy again.

But apparently George was still not quite happy.

'I don't understand you,' he said. 'You talk about it so calmly—as if there were nothing blameworthy in being divorced, as if there were nothing unusual in my marrying a divorced woman, as if there were nothing wrong in our having lived together for years without having been married.'

Very simply, very touchingly, Olivia announced her creed.

'What seems wrong to me is that I lived for five years with a bad man whom I hated. What seems right to me is that I lived for five years with a good man whom I love.'

Tenderly she held out her hand to him: to her friend, to the good man she loved. He took it, patted it ... but could come no nearer to her.

'Yes, yes, my dear,' he said, as if explaining to a child. 'But right and wrong don't settle themselves as easily as that. We've been living together when you were Telworthy's wife. That's wrong.'

She withdrew her hand, and said coolly, 'Do you mean wicked?'

'Well, no doubt,' he hedged, 'the court would consider that we acted in perfect innocence—'

In a hard cold voice which he had never heard from her before, she asked, 'What court?' He blundered on.

'These things would have to be done legally, of course. I believe the proper method is a nullity suit, declaring our marriage null and—er—void. It would, so to speak, wipe out these years of—er—'

'Wickedness?'

'Of irregular union, and—er—then—' He hesitated, and she finished the sentence for him.

'Then I could go back to Jacob.' She turned to him, so that he should see her full face, and asked, a note of warning in her voice, 'Do you really mean that, George?'

He shifted uncomfortably.

'Well, dear, you see—that's how things are—one can't get away from the facts.'

'Yes, let us keep to the facts. I want this quite clear, so that there can be no mistake about it.' She was silent for a moment, thinking how best to put it. 'What you feel is that Telworthy has the greater claim? Is that right? You are prepared to—to make way for him?'

He did not answer directly, but the most direct answer could not have been more clear.

'Both the Church and the Law would say that I had no claim at all, I'm afraid. Well, I—I suppose I haven't.'

'I see.' She looked at him gravely for a while. Then gave a little nod of understanding. 'Thank you for making it so clear to me.'

So it happened that way after all. The unbelievable was true. He was prepared to let her go, a, sacrifice to the high gods of Propriety. Even in these last few minutes, while the shadow of its coming was growing darker and darker, she had refused to believe it. But now it was true.

If he had only given her one word of love, given her one speech to show that he felt for her, no less than for himself! But he had said nothing. The scandal, the immorality, his mind was full of these only. Even the fact that their happy fife together was to end now was of less importance to him than the fact (as he regarded it) that their life together had been immoral. If he had cried passionately, 'I *can't* let you go!—and yet I must!' ah! how she would have warmed to him, how she would have stretched out her arms to him, so foolish to say 'I must,' so dear to say 'I can't.' No, it was not his narrowness which hurt her, his rigid 'I must'; it was the seeming absence of hurt to him; it was the ease with which he let her go.

Yet he loved her; she was sure of that. It was only that he lacked imagination. He had not seen himself alone again at Marden House, he had not seen his wife, Olivia, back again with Telworthy. His mind travelled so slowly. Well, he should see it. She was not his wife any more? She belonged to Telworthy now? Very well, then she was not his wife any more. Now, George, see how you like it.

She stole a glance at him, and smiled. They were coming from generalities to particularities. Poor George! What a shock it would be for him.

'Of course,' he said, speaking his thoughts aloud, 'whether or not you go back to—er—Telworthy is another matter altogether. That would naturally be for you to decide.'

Olivia nodded.

'For me and Jacko to decide,' she said cheerfully.

He turned a blank face towards her.

'Jacko?'

She gave him a bright little smile.

'Yes. I used to call my first husband—I mean, of course, my only husband—Jacko. I didn't like the name of Jacob, and Jacko seemed to suit him somehow—he had very long arms.' She laughed happily, reminiscently, an intimate laugh which excluded George from any share in the joke. 'Dear Jacko!'

'You don't seem to realize that this is not a joke,' he said stiffly.

'It may not be a joke, but it *is* funny, isn't it?'

'I am bound to say that I do not see anything funny in a tragedy which has wrecked two lives.'

She flashed a glance at him. Ah, he was coming to it at last. But she pretended to misunderstand him.

'Two lives? Oh, but Jacko's life isn't wrecked.' She laughed. 'It has just been miraculously restored to him. And a wife, too. Oh, there's nothing tragic for Jacko in it.'

'I was referring to *our* two lives,' said George very coldly. 'Yours and mine.'

She could not keep the bitterness of it out of her voice as she answered: 'Yours, George? Your life isn't wrecked. The court will absolve you of all blame; your friends will sympathize with you, and tell you that I was a designing woman who deliberately took you in; your Aunt Julia—'

'Stop it!'

The cry burst from him, and she stopped on the word, so that there was a moment of utter silence, before he went on, grumbling, arguing with himself rather than with her: 'What do you mean? Have you no heart? Do you think I want to lose you, Olivia? Do you think I want my home broken up like this?' And then pathetically: 'Haven't you been happy with me these last five years?'

'Very happy,' she breathed softly.

'Well, then! How can you talk like that?'

'But you want to send me away,' she murmured.

'There you go again!' He flung out a complaining hand at her. 'I don't *want* to. I have hardly had time to realize yet what it will mean to me when you go. The fact is, I simply daren't realize it. I daren't think about it.'

And that was just the truth, that was just the trouble. Very slowly, very earnestly, she said:

'*Try* thinking about it, George.'

'And you talk as if I *wanted* to send you away,' he grumbled.

'Try *thinking* about it, George,' she said again.

But he went on with his grievance. 'You don't seem to understand that I'm not *sending* you away. You simply aren't mine to keep.'

'Whose am I?' she asked, surprised.

'Your husband's—Telworthy's.'

She shook her head with a little smile.

'If I belong to anybody but myself, I think I belong to you, George.'

But he would not have her.

'Not in the eyes of the Law,' he said. 'Not in the eyes of the Church. Not even in the eyes of—er—'

'The County?' she prompted.

He answered her with some dignity that he had been about to say 'Heaven.' Olivia gave a little shrug. After all, there was not much difference.

'Oh, that this should happen to *us*!' he burst out again, shaking his clenched fists at the Providence which had allowed it. To us! He meant 'to us Mardens.' That was the amazing thing. What was coming to the world?

Olivia followed him with her eyes as he walked up and down the room. He had failed her; whatever happened now, she could never quite forget that. Let the Law and the Church, Heaven or the County rule him as it will, there was something which he ought to have said to her first. Whatever was right, whatever was wrong, there was something which he ought to have said to her. However bad it was for him, it was worse for her, and she should have come first into his mind. 'Olivia, I can't let you go!' But he had not said it.

Was there still time to make him see where he was going? She would try again. She shook out the curtains, looked at them with her head on one side, and said, 'I do hope Jacko will like these.'

He wheeled round on her in amazement. Hands stretched towards her he cried, 'Olivia, Olivia, have you no heart?'

He to ask her that!

She answered flippantly: 'Ought you to talk like that to another man's wife?'

'Confound it,' he said, really annoyed now, 'is this just a joke to you?'

'You must forgive me, George. I am a little overexcited. At the thought of returning to Jacko, no doubt. '

'Do you *want* to return to him?' he asked jealously. Yes, jealousy, at last! With what gladness she heard and registered that note.

'One wants to do what is right,' she said meekly, 'in the eyes of—er—Heaven.'

'Seeing what sort of man he is, I have no doubt that you could get a separation, supposing that he didn't—er—divorce you.' He shook his head in a dazed way over the problems in front of them. 'I don't know, I don't know.'

And then suddenly a gleam of sunshine pierced the black clouds which enveloped him. His eyes brightened. All was not yet lost.

'I must consult my solicitor,' he said, relief in his voice.

'Wouldn't you like to consult your Aunt Julia, too?' suggested Olivia. 'She could tell you what the County—I mean, what Heaven really thought about it.'

'Yes, you're quite right. Aunt Julia has plenty of common sense. Her advice—'

'Do I still call her *Aunt* Julia?' Olivia wondered.

He stared at her. 'Why ever not?'

She looked at him with a smile. He was still refusing to 'think about it.' He was to do the right thing in the eyes of his gods; the home was to be broken up, she was to go back to Telworthy; but somehow she was still pouring out his coffee for him in the morning. In some curious way Lady Marden was still Mrs. Telworthy's aunt. 'Try thinking about it, George!'

Under her smile he stammered that of course—er—yes, that was so, but—well, they needn't bother about that. The main point was that Aunt Julia's advice would be invaluable. She must certainly be told; now.

'And Mr. Pim, George? He will have to know.'

'I don't see the necessity.'

'Not even for me? When a woman suddenly hears that her long-lost husband is restored to her, don't you think that she wants to ask questions?'

'Questions?'

Of course!' She rattled off the questions gaily. 'How is he looking, and where is he living, and when is he—'

'I suppose if you are interested in these things—'

'Don't be so silly, George! How can I help being? Naturally I must know what Jacko—'

An ejaculation of some sort escaped him, and she stopped, waiting for it to become more articulate.

'Yes?' she helped him.

'I wish you wouldn't call him by that ridiculous name,' he growled.

She looked away from him. 'My husband, then,' she amended quietly.

He winced at the word. 'Well?'

'Well, we must know my husband's plans—where we can communicate with him, and so on.'

'I have no wish to communicate with him,' he said with dignity.

'I'm afraid you will have to, dear.'

Once more he replied that he didn't see the necessity.

She bent down more closely over her curtains to hide a smile.

'Well,' she said, 'you will want to—to apologize to him for living with his wife for so long.' She stole a glance at him, and went on. 'And since I belong to him, he ought to be told where he can call for me.'

Nobody had a better sense of humour than George; he had often said so. But this was not the time for humour. His dignified answer that there was some truth in what she said was sufficient reproof. Yes, undoubtedly Telworthy would have to be seen. Or perhaps—happy thought—his solicitors could do it all.

'But oh!' he groaned, 'the horrible publicity of it.'

And Olivia felt for him, even though he was hurting her so much. Publicity! She knew all about that. Her first husband, her only husband, could have told George something of the disadvantage of publicity. He had fled from it to Australia; even when there it would not leave him alone. Yes, there had been enough 'Telworthy' in the papers for Jacob, enough for Olivia. Now she was to have it again. Yet how trivial it was all compared with the one fact which mattered, that George was sending her away. How trivial to her—but how terrifying to George.

She got up and went over to him.

'Dear, don't think that I don't sympathize with you,' she said, and if there was the least little hint of irony in her words he did not notice it. 'I understand so exactly how you're feeling about it. The publicity! Yes, it is terrible.'

He took her hand and looked at her earnestly.

'I want to do what is right, Olivia,' he said. 'You believe that?'

'Of course I do.'

He thanked her with his eyes, gravely, and let her go. She gave a rueful little smile, and added, 'It is only that we don't quite agree as to what is right and what is wrong.'

'It isn't a question of agreeing,' he reproved her. 'Right is right and wrong is wrong all the world over.'

'But more particularly in Buckinghamshire, I think,' she said with a sigh.

He did not hear her. He went on, arguing the matter out to himself. 'If I only considered myself, I should say "Let us pack this man Telworthy back to Australia. He will make no claim; he will accept money to go away and say nothing about it." If I only consulted my own happiness, that is what I would say, Olivia.'

Oh, why had he not spoken like that at first! Eagerly she leant towards him, her hands clasped, entreating him with her eyes, with every line of her body, to be true to the love which she had given him; to take her in his arms now, and say defiantly—

But no. That was not George. George went on heavily, 'But when I consult my conscience—'

His happiness! *His* conscience! Never hers.

'When I consult my conscience, then I can't do it. It's wrong!'

He said it nobly, finely, the good man obeying his conscience and therefore sure of himself. And yet, what is a man's conscience after all? That inner voice which whispers to us 'No, you mustn't do it; it's wrong'; that voice which, if disobeyed, reproaches us, leaves us with an uneasy sense of guilt, is it always an inspired voice? Is it the voice of the God within us? Or is it only the voice of those who taught us in our childhood; not the voice of truth, but of what others thought true? Sometimes no more than that.

His conscience! That ended the argument. It told Olivia that he would not 'try thinking about it' himself, but would accept what had been thought about it by others.

Chapter Ten

A Family Council

I

Lady Marden was what Brian called 'good at pigs.' She had the manner. Brian was quite frankly 'no good at pigs.' He was a poor eighteen, and Lady Marden was plus four, and Dinah, he estimated, was about six, having begun young, but never having kept it up properly.

To be bad at anything does not mean that you are bored by it. Brian was as interested in the pigs as he was in everything which made up this wonderful life. He liked watching them with Dinah, and encouraging the younger members of the family, and scratching their backs, and discovering likenesses in their innocent faces to various eminent authors, politicians or painters. It was a fleeting resemblance to a prominent statesman which had first endeared Arnold, the little black-and-white one, to him and Dinah. They had christened him Arnold before the likeness had struck them; otherwise his name would have been—but that doesn't matter.

They accompanied Aunt Julia to the farm, these two children, in the absurdest spirits, one on each side of her. Now and then Brian's left hand would stray behind Aunt Julia's back, as if he intended to embrace her, but it was Dinah's right hand which stole out to meet it, the while they looked straight in front of them, as though discerning some unusual object on the horizon, or answered some question of the grown-up's in an unnecessarily eager voice. Then they would catch each other's eyes, and Dinah would laugh her wonderful laugh, much to Aunt Julia's amazement, and Brian's giggle would fade into a bronchial irritation under a sudden head-turn and a stare of cold surprise.

'So you paint, Mr.—what's your name?' said Lady Marden.

'Mr. Strange, Aunt Julia,' said Dinah kindly. 'Brian Strange, the well-known painter. You must have heard of him.'

Brian pulled at his tie with the idea of improving himself into somebody of whom everybody had heard.

'H'm! Can't say I have. What do you paint?'

'Oh, well—'

'He sold a picture last March for fifty pounds,' put in the faithful Dinah, determined to make this quite clear.

'What was it called?'

'The World's End: Saturday Night,' said Brian, glad to explain it so easily. No artist but hates talking of his work to those who neither understand nor take any interest, and it is fortunate for us all that the inquirer is so completely satisfied with the mere title of the great work. When once you have told the visitor that the new comedy is called 'Collusion' or 'Agatha' or any other name you like to invent for the occasion, the danger is over, and you can pass on to the wickedness of the poorer classes.

But, of course, if you deliberately choose a challenging title, you must expect them to comment on it.

'I see. A religious picture. And so the world's going to end on a Saturday night, Mr. Strange? Well, I dare say you're right, but I don't know who told you.'

Brian explained that 'The World's End' was the name of a public-house near his studio.

Lady Marden nodded unabashed.

'My acquaintance with public-houses is small. You must forgive me, Mr. Strange, for not having heard of yours.'

'Not at all,' said Brian politely.

'And do you paint yours from the inside or the outside?'

Brian signalled to Dinah the impossibility of carrying on this kind of conversation, and resigned his share in it to her.

'It isn't just the public-house, Aunt Julia,' she explained enthusiastically. 'It's where the buses stop, and Brian's picture is an impression of the street on a wet Saturday night, with hawkers shouting at their barrows, and the lights flaring and dropping in great splashes on the puddles, and—oh, it's wonderful!'

The author of it looked supremely uncomfortable, and frowned at his press-agent, begging her not to waste all this on the Philistines. But Aunt Julia had only heard one word of it.

'*Whose* picture?' she asked sternly.

'Brian's,' repeated Dinah calmly.

'Ah!' said Aunt Julia. She looked from one to the other of them, read their secret, and strode grimly on towards the pigs.

But for once her inspection of them was undistinguished. She might have been the merest novice; all that good meat was wasted on her, whose mind was busy with another stock. The Mardens. Here was Dinah, with the taint of the poet already in her, suggesting that she should be crossed with an artist! True, the result would not be called Marden, but it would be in the family. What on earth was George about?

She did not say it aloud; perhaps she did not think it in those very words, but that was the sense of her thoughts as she leant over the sty and inhaled the little pigs. Dinah, of all the Marden girls that ever stepped, needed careful marrying. Only an honest, patriotic, well-tubbed, sport-loving, beef-and-beer Englishman could save her. Lady Marden decided that she must have a few words alone with George on this subject before she left. Perhaps a few words of warning to Mr. Strange first would not be out of place.

II

Olivia, the curtains on her lap and in her hands, her eyes looking into nothingness; George at his desk, head bowed on arms; as soon as she came into the morning-room Dinah saw that something more than an investment had gone wrong with these.

'Hallo!' she said.

George looked at her stupidly for a moment.

'Where's Aunt Julia?' asked Olivia, coming back with a little shake to her curtains.

'Talking to Brian. I was sent on, because it wasn't considered proper for me to listen. I expect she's asking him to paint her portrait. As Diana. Surprised bathing.'

'Can you find her, dear, and bring her here? And Brian, too. We have something we want to talk about with you all.'

This was too much for George.

'Olivia!' he protested.

'Right-o!' said Dinah. And then, as she went out, 'What fun!' For things were indeed occurring now at Marden House— at Marden House, where, as she had told Mr. Pim only that morning, 'nothing ever happened.' What fun when they did happen!

But it was still too much for George.

'Olivia,' he protested again, 'you don't seriously suggest that we should discuss these things with a child like Dinah, and a young man like Strange, a mere acquaintance?'

'Dinah will have to know, my dear,' she said, shaking her head with a little smile at him; a sad little smile for the way he went on refusing to think about it. 'I am very fond of Dinah, you know. You can't send me away without telling Dinah. And Brian is *my* friend. You have your solicitor and your aunt and your conscience to consult—mayn't I even have Brian?'

George had not thought of that. He had thought of nothing but the catastrophe as it affected *him*, never as it affected her.

He saw dimly now that it was her catastrophe, too. Yet to whom does a good woman go in time of trouble?

'I should have thought your husband —'

'Yes, but we don't know where Jacko is,' said Olivia.

'I was not referring to Telworthy,' he stuttered.

'Well, then?' Her hands and eyes finished the question. To whom?

He struggled on. Naturally his advice, his assistance was— that is, she wasn't to think that—he meant that even if he wasn't legally her husband—that is to say—and then, head in arms again, 'Oh, this is horrible!'

It was so that Aunt Julia found him. She looked at him in astonishment. Could a man so well-aired, so well-exercised as George break down like this? It seemed impossible. And certainly impossible as a result of Dinah's foolishness only. Anger, yes, at that foolishness; scorn, if you like; but not despair. What had happened?

Brian wondered, too. But when you are twenty-four, and have just found that the biggest darling in the world loves you, the troubles of a man in the forties do not seem to amount to much. Anyway, Brian had despaired of George a long time ago, so that there were plenty of reasons why George should now despair of himself. Still, something had evidently happened.

Olivia took charge.

'George and I have had some rather bad news, Aunt Julia,' she said, as she got up. 'He wanted your advice. Where will you sit?'

'Thank you, Olivia, I can sit down by myself.'

No fussing for Aunt Julia, no pampering. She sat down by herself, removing a degenerate cushion first. Dinah hurried to Olivia's side. Brian leant against the back of the sofa, within reach of Dinah. They waited eagerly.

'Well,' said Aunt Julia, after a long silence, 'what is it?' And then, as there was no answer, 'Money, I suppose. Nobody's safe nowadays.'

123

It was for George to say, but he was obviously incapable. He began, once, twice, and then signalled to Olivia. She told them quite simply; it was not the sort of news which you could break.

'We've just heard that my first husband is still alive.'

They exclaimed in their different fashions. 'Good Lord!' said Brian, and looked from one to the other of them. Lady Marden looked at her nephew only. 'George!' she cried, horrified that he could have let this happen. 'Telworthy!' said Dinah, in awe, adding excitedly, 'And only this morning I was saying that nothing ever happened in this house.' But she did not wait for Olivia's reproachful look. She had her arm round the beloved one in a moment, murmuring 'Darling, I don't mean that! Darling one!' and was forgiven.

'What does this mean, George?' asked his Aunt Julia sternly. 'I leave you for ten minutes, barely ten minutes, to go and look at the pigs, and when I come back you tell me that Olivia is a bigamist.'

That ugly word 'bigamist' stabbed Brian. And there was that in Lady Marden's voice which made it clear that there was to be no sympathy with Olivia in George's family. He shot up to protest, but Olivia put out a hand and held him back. He pressed the hand, assuring her in his boyish way that if there was a row, he was on her side. Her eyes thanked him.

'Well, George?' said his aunt.

The unhappy man roused himself.

'I'm afraid it is true, Aunt Julia,' he admitted wearily. 'We heard the news just before lunch, just before you came. We've only this moment had an opportunity of talking about it, of wondering what to do.'

'What was his name? Tel—something.'

'Jacob Telworthy.'

'So he's alive still?'

'Apparently. There seems to be no doubt about it.'

Lady Marden, if we may use the word, grunted. Then she turned to the prisoner in the dock, and said:

'Didn't you *see* him die? I should always want to *see* my husband die before I married again. Not that I approve of second marriages, anyhow.' Then back to her nephew, 'I told you so at the time, George.'

'And me, Aunt Julia,' put in Olivia quietly.

But Lady Marden was not at all abashed.

'Did I? Well, I generally say what I think.'

George remembered that the prisoner in the dock was his wife. Well, no, not his wife, but at least a woman, and that he was an English gentleman.

'I ought to tell you, Aunt Julia,' he said, 'that no blame attaches to Olivia over this. Of that I am perfectly satisfied. It's nobody's fault.'

'Except Telworthy's,' said Lady Marden, heavily sarcastic. 'He seems to have been rather careless. Well, what are you going to do about it?'

'That's just it. It's a terrible situation. There's bound to be so much publicity.'

Lady Marden shuddered.

'Not only all this,' he went on, 'but—but Telworthy's past and everything.'

'His past?' said his aunt, frowning her amazement. 'I should have said that it was his present which was the trouble. Had he a past as well?'

George looked miserably at Olivia.

'He was a fraudulent company-promoter,' explained Olivia calmly. 'He went to prison a good deal.'

There was a moment of consternation, while the three of them who were hearing the news for the first time tried to realize what it meant. Brian's imagination lit up for him, in a flash, the whole of Olivia's life. Once again he wondered at women; their capability of suffering, their courage, their power of coming

125

through. And to come through so untouched! He looked at Olivia reverently. Was Dinah equally a woman, he wondered. Was she bringing him an equal courage, an equal steadfastness? His heart glowed with pride. Impossible to doubt it.

And Dinah put her arms round Olivia. What did it matter whom Olivia had married that first time? Why shouldn't her husband be a fraudulent what-d'you-call-it and go to prison? She was Olivia just the same. Let who dared say anything against her!

But Lady Marden had no eyes for the prisoner in the dock. There had never been any hope for Olivia. But that George should so offend!

'George,' she said grimly, 'you never told me this.'

George stuttered. He had deceived himself for so long that he was still uncertain whether he had really known about Jacob Telworthy at the time of his engagement to Olivia. But even if he hadn't known, his Aunt Julia would say that he ought to have known; and if he had known, he ought to have told her; so that in any case—

Indignantly Dinah broke in.

'What's it got to do with Olivia, anyhow?' she demanded fiercely. 'It's not her fault.'

'Oh no,' said Aunt Julia, sarcastic again, 'I dare say it's mine.'

Olivia shuddered. They were wrangling. How horrible! She tried to get them back.

'George,' she said gently, 'you wanted to ask Aunt Julia what was the best thing to do.'

This was too much for Brian. He jumped up, breathing amazement, scorn, anger. 'Good heavens!' he cried. 'What *is* there to do except the one and only thing?' Then, conscious suddenly that he was taking the floor, realizing that in any case he had no footing in a family discussion, with a horrible feeling that he was going to be melodramatic directly, he ended up lamely, 'I beg your pardon. You don't want me to—er—'

'*I* do, Brian,' said Olivia gently.

'Well, go on, Mr. Strange,' said Lady Marden, with a shrug. 'What would *you* do in George's position?'

'Do?' said Brian, thrusting his head forward. 'Say to the woman I love, "You're mine! And let this other damned fellow come and take you from me if he can!" And he couldn't—how could he?' his boyish voice rang out triumphantly. 'Not if the woman chose *me*!'

A little sigh escaped Olivia. At last she had heard the words for which she had been waiting. 'You're mine—and let this other damned fellow come and take you from me if he can.' Ah, why did George not say them? Was it too much to expect? Were they very difficult words to say? But George had not said them. He had had to wait for Brian, the boy whom he despised, to tell him what to say. Thank you, Brian. Now you have told him. Was I so very unreasonable?

But Dinah had never heard that ring in Brian's voice before. She knew him so well to talk to, to laugh with; all the surface Brian, the Brian which the world saw, she knew and loved, but the other Brian, the underneath Brian, was a stranger. Just for a moment he had peeped out, that stammering moment, when a voice she did not know said for the first time, 'I love you,' but after that first fierce kiss, he had withdrawn once more into his fastness. And now he was out again; and he and all the other Brians were hers!

'Oh, Brian,' she whispered, looking at him adoringly. She clung to his arm. And then, just for the joy of hearing him say it, yet to be quite certain also, she added, 'It *is* me, isn't it, and not Olivia?' And he came back from the imaginary Dinah, whom he was defending from a hundred imaginary foes, to the real Dinah who was looking so wistfully at him, and said tenderly, 'You baby! Of course!' She nodded to herself, happily. Yes, it was she.

There was an angry flush on George's cheek. He writhed under the unfairness of putting up this boy to say the fine, the romantic thing against him. Damnably unfair! It was so easy to be fine, to make a gesture of chivalry and to let your duty go. Of course he, George, wanted to say, 'You're mine!' to Olivia; anybody in his place would, anybody who loved Olivia as much as he loved her; and if he had cared nothing for his duty, nothing for morality, he would have said it. Yes; taken her in his arms and said it; it was easy enough. And that damned boy, barely out of school, thinks he can come along and tell him, George Marden, how to love a woman! Perhaps he would find out himself some day, if he ever grew up, that life was not so easy as that. 'You're mine'—that was just it, she wasn't his, not if the laws of God and man meant anything. And Dinah was to marry a fellow like that!

Lady Marden, wondering where young men like Mr. Strange came from, but realizing that in these days there were all sorts of curious people in the world, let him down gently with, 'I am afraid, young man, that your morals are as peculiar as your views on art.'

'This is not a question of morals, or of art,' said Brian hotly. 'It's a question of love.'

'Hear, hear!' agreed Dinah.

Lady Marden turned in surprise to her nephew.

'Isn't it that girl's bedtime?' she asked.

Olivia, with a tender reproving smile at the girl, said that they would let her sit up a little longer if she were good.

'I will be good, Olivia,' she protested. 'But I thought anybody, however important a debate was, was allowed to say "Hear, hear!"'

George, still glowering at Brian, said coldly that if they were going to discuss the matter seriously, Mr. Strange had better take Dinah outside.

'Strange, if you—er—'

'Tell them what you have settled first,' said Olivia quietly.

'Settled?' quoth Lady Marden. 'What is there to settle? It settles itself.'

George, shame-faced, miserable, acknowledged his agreement. That was just it. The laws of God and Man, Duty, Right, Conscience, all had settled it.

'The marriage must be annulled,' went on Lady Marden, interpreting Right to the uninitiated. 'Annulled, I think that is the word, George?'

George presumed it was.

'One's solicitor will know all about that, of course.'

There was just a flicker of brightness on George's face at the word 'solicitor'. Helpful fellows, solicitors. He nodded, 'Yes.'

'And then?' asked Brian challengingly.

'Presumably,' said Aunt Julia, 'Olivia will return to her lawful husband.'

Brian's scornful laugh rang out. 'And that's morality!' he cried. And with his boyish undisciplined contempt for all that these people stood for, he added, 'As expounded by Bishop Landseer!'

The contempt in his voice was too much for George. He strode over to Brian and looked him up and down.

'I don't know what you mean by Bishop Landseer,' he said angrily, 'but I can tell you this. Morality means acting in accordance with the laws of the land and the laws of the Church. I am quite prepared to believe that your creed embraces neither marriage nor monogamy, but my creed is different.'

'My creed includes both marriage and monogamy,' answered Brian in a high, excited voice, 'and monogamy means sticking to the woman you love as long as she wants you.'

George turned away with a contemptuous snort. But Lady Marden said calmly, 'Apparently, Mr. Strange, you suggest that George and Olivia should go on living together, although they have never been legally married, and wait for this man Telworthy to divorce her. Why, bless the man! What do you think the County would say?'

A scornful laugh was all that Brian had for the County.

'Well, if you really want to know,' answered Dinah unexpectedly, 'the men would say, "Gad! she's a fine woman, I don't wonder he sticks to her," and the women would say, "I can't think what he sees in her to stick to her like that," and they'd all say, "Well, after all, he may be a damn fool, but you can't deny he's a sportsman."' Breathlessly she rattled it off, and ended with a triumphant '*That's* what the County would say.'

The 'damn fool' was too much for George Marden.

'Was it for this sort of thing,' he said furiously to Olivia, 'that you insisted on having Dinah and Mr. Strange in here? To insult me in my own house?'

Aunt Julia said she couldn't think what young people were coming to in these days. Possibly lack of healthy exercise accounted for it in Mr. Strange's case, but the girl had been properly brought up

'Just at the moment,' explained her nephew, 'she thinks she is in love with Mr. Strange. I give no countenance whatever to the idea—'

'Naturally.'

How horrible this family wrangle was! Olivia, wincing at it, pressed Dinah's hand and said that she and Brian had better go. Dinah stood up.

'We will go, Olivia.' She went up to her uncle. 'But I'm just going to say one thing, Uncle George. Brian and I *are* going to marry each other, and when we are married, we'll stick to each other—how*ever* many of our dead husbands and wives turn up!'

And with this all-embracing statement of her faith, she called, 'Come on, Brian,' to her lover, and strode from the room.

II

A nullity suit! It was the only way. But the horrible publicity of it! Photographs of Olivia, of himself, of Telworthy, in every paper. Telworthy's past history raked up. Strident paper-boys shouting, 'Marden Case, Latest,' in the London streets. People opening their papers in the tube and trains and trams as they went home; commenting on it to each other, 'Rum thing, this Marden Case.' His neighbours' tactful sympathy in front of him, their busy gossip behind his back. Their servants, his own servants, full of it, but showing impassive faces to him ... And this morning he had been happy!

'I don't remember anything of the sort in the Marden family before,' said Aunt Julia. 'Ever!' She looked gloomily at Olivia, who had done it, and repeated, 'Ever!'

In some queer way George felt suddenly that this was unfair to Olivia; he resented it. He was as tender of the Marden name as Aunt Julia, but there was that one blot on it, and in fairness to Olivia he could not let it be forgotten now. He glanced across at his aunt and murmured:

'Lady Fanny.'

It seemed to him odd that he should have been looking at her portrait, and thinking about her, only that morning. It was not odd really, because he saw her every day at breakfast and, since most of his thoughts were as much a matter of routine as his actions, thought about her in consequence every day. She had run away with young Buckhurst, had been happy with him from all accounts, in spite of her wickedness. But from that day the Mardens had had no word for her; or but one word only, more suited to her time than to George's. Yet George liked looking at her, she was so beautiful—almost as beautiful as Olivia.

'Yes, yes, of course,' acknowledged Lady Marden hastily. 'But that was two hundred years ago. And, of course,' she comforted herself, 'the standards were different then. Besides, it wasn't quite the same.'

'No,' agreed George absently, 'it wasn't the same.'

Not the same. No Marden had been so cruelly treated as he.

He looked across at Olivia. There she sat, waiting. There was nothing which she could do now, nor say. It was for him to fight it out for himself. And looking at her, so dear, so beautiful, he began for the first time to 'think about it.' He was sending her away! And when she was gone—

He tried to imagine her gone. Absurdly he saw her suddenly in relation to Lumsden; Lumsden down at the farm, talking business to him, but ever including Olivia in an affectionate, 'You see, madam,' as if it were *her* approval which he was really seeking to win. There she stood, by his side, her skirt rippling gently in the wind, one arm raised to her hat, and that friendliness in her eyes which none could resist. They went to the dairy, the stables, they spoke to a gamekeeper or a gardener; it was always the same; she was their lady. How easy yesterday to do all this business alone, as so often he had done it alone; how hard to-morrow to do it alone, knowing that she would never come with him again, as so often she had come? Oh, Olivia, Olivia! What was he to do?

'If there were any other way!' he groaned. 'Olivia, what *can* I do?' He went up to her, pleading, apologizing, justifying himself. 'It *is* the only way, isn't it? All that that fellow said—of course, it sounds very well, but as things are—' He gave a despairing shrug. 'Is there anything in marriage, or isn't there? You believe that there is, don't you? You aren't one of these Socialists? Well, then, *can* we go on living together when you're another man's wife? It isn't only what other people will say, but it *is* wrong, isn't it?'

He was a child now, asking for help from its mother; she so wise, so understanding, she will tell him. 'It *is* wrong, isn't it?' he pleaded.

She did not take her eyes off him. He could not escape her eyes. He might look down, or look away, but he had to come back to them.

'And supposing he doesn't divorce you,' he went on, 'are we to go on living together, unmarried, for ever?'

Her eyes were still there. He saw reflected in them the accusation in his own soul.

'Olivia,' he protested, 'you seem to think that I'm just thinking of the publicity; of what people will say. I'm not! I'm not! That comes in anyway, now. But I want to do what's right, what's best. I don't mean what's best for *us*, what makes us happiest; I mean what's really best, what's—what's Tightest.'

He stopped and mumbled, 'What anybody else would do in my place.'

Her eyes were still there.

'Oh, Olivia,' he burst out, 'it's so unfair! *I* don't know. You're not my wife at all, but I want to do what's right.' And then, desperate, he met her eyes, and, holding out his hands to her, cried, 'Oh, Olivia, Olivia, you do understand, don't you?'

Without moving, without taking her eyes from his, she answered tenderly, gently, as if breathing her thoughts aloud:

'So very, very well, my dear. I understand just what you are feeling. And oh, I do so wish that you could—' She broke off, leaving the wish unexpressed, and added with a little sigh: 'But then, that wouldn't be George. Not the George I married.' With a rueful little laugh she corrected herself, 'Or didn't quite marry.'

They had forgotten Lady Marden. She existed for them no longer. She tried to recall them to their surroundings by saying that they were both talking a little wildly, but she said it half-heartedly, as if she knew that she counted for nothing now. They did not hear her.

'Or—didn't—quite—marry,' whispered Olivia again, so tenderly, so pathetically, so beseechingly, all her soul in her dear eyes, calling to him to come to her, to make her with one kiss his wife again. Or didn't quite marry? There was a question in it for him, to which, now for ever, he must give the answer. She was there, to take or to refuse …

Which would he have done? He tried to look away from her, but she held his eyes. This was his last chance. Desperately he wrestled with himself. Was anything right, was anything wrong, when she looked at him like that. Olivia, I can't let you go—he was saying it at last. Olivia, I must let you go—ah, but would he now? His hands begin to go out to her. Olivia! Slowly she begins to stand up, calling him, calling him still. Will he take her?

But at that moment Anne came in.

'Mr. Pim is here, sir,' she announced.

Chapter Eleven

A Dispensation of Providence

I

Mr. Pim had left Marden House with the pleasant feeling that his story had gone well. What a charming and successful morning it had been! The Mardens, so kind, so hospitable; the girl—what was her name?—Diana—so young, so fresh; and then that handsome boy, so easy, so well-mannered. There were no people like the English. And the atmosphere of the country-house, quiet, sunny, well-ordered, where else but in England could you find it? It was good to be home again.

He made his way happily to the Trevors', humming to himself. In his pocket was the letter of introduction to Fanshawe; that was good. He had telegraphed to dear Prudence; that was good also. He must try not to forget the flowers for her. She was so fond of flowers. He stopped for a moment, taking off his hat to let the kindly summer morning play round his bare head. Was there ever a more perfect day? Warm, yet not too warm. He looked up to the sky, thanking whatever gods there be for the happiness which they had given him in this world. 'And quite frankly,' he added aloud, 'I do not see how the next world, if indeed there is a next world, can be more beautiful than this morning, though it may be we shall be better able to appreciate it.'

At lunch he told his story again, seated between Trevor and his wife. They listened with smiles on their faces for each other and for him. 'What a dear old man he is,' said her eyes.

'A bad fellow he had been, Mrs. Trevor, I'm afraid. But no worse than many of us, I dare say. Now, what *was* his name? Dear me, I ought to remember it. Rather a peculiar one.'

They waited for him to remember it. Then, seeing his difficulty, Mrs. Trevor pressed some more coffee on him, and in his courteous refusal of it the story drifted away. Resting in the garden afterwards, Mrs. Pim thought again with pleasure of his visit to the Mardens. How interested they had been in his adventures! The Trevors, too. A pity he had forgotten the name. Now, what *was* it?

He was roused from his thoughts by George's messenger. Mrs. Trevor's permission granted, he opened the letter and read it twice; first to himself, and then with a preliminary, 'Now this is very curious,' to his hostess.

'Very curious,' he repeated. 'But, of course, I will go.'

'Perhaps your Mr. Fanshawe is out of England, and George has just remembered it, and wants to give you a letter to somebody else,' suggested Mrs. Trevor.

Mr. Pim nodded gently at her.

'No doubt that will be it.' He turned out his pockets, came across the unposted letter to his sister again, looked at it reproachfully, smiled as he remembered that he had already dealt with it, picked out George's letter to Fanshawe, and said again as he contemplated it: 'Yes, no doubt that will be the case.' He stood up and held out his hand to her. 'Good-bye, Mrs. Trevor. Let me thank you for your hospitality to an old man, and Mr. Trevor also. I shall take back to London with me very pleasant memories of my little visit to your corner of the world where you have all been so kind to me.'

'You must come down again, Mr. Pim,' said Trevor heartily. 'We shall look forward to seeing you when you are next this way.'

'Thank you, thank you!'

'Good-bye, Mr. Pim,' said his hostess, smiling affectionately at him, 'it has been so nice to have you.'

Trevor saw him safely into George's trap and came back to his wife. They looked at each other without speaking for a moment.

Then Trevor said, a little shame-faced:

'He's like a summer Sunday evening with church bells in the distance.'

Which may not have been an exact description of Mr. Pim, but was certainly not bad for Jack Trevor.

II

The announcement that Mr. Pim was here brought George and Olivia slowly back to their surroundings.

'Mr. Pim?' said George, blankly at first, and he stared at Anne, wondering how she had come there.

'Mr. Pim, dear. Show Mr. Pim in here, please, Anne.'

'Yes, madam.'

She went out, modest, quiet, correct, but with a 'Well, I never did!' stowed away in the back of her mind until such moment as she was off duty again, and could communicate freely with her equals. Olivia, who was in control of herself again, had a moment in which to wonder how much Anne had seen, but George neither wondered nor, wondering, would have minded. Anne, he would have told himself, was the last person to discuss him with her fellow-servants. Even if he had heard her doing so, he would not have recognized it, for he did not know that there were two Annes, each with an appropriate voice.

Lady Marden recalled herself again to their attention.

'Who on earth is Mr. Pim?' she demanded of her nephew.

He had dropped into a chair, out of breath with his emotion, and was blowing his nose loudly in the search for calm. Olivia, herself busy with a handkerchief, explained the approaching visitor to Lady Marden.

'I see.' Then reluctantly she asked: 'Shall I be in the way?'

Olivia looked across at George. He shrugged his shoulders indifferently.

'Please stay,' said Olivia, and Aunt Julia stayed firmly.

Mr. Pim was announced. He came in, smiles ready for his old friends the Mardens, apologies on his lips for the trouble he was giving them in this matter of the letter of introduction.

'Ah, Mr. Pim!' said George, 'Very good of you to come. The fact is—er—'

It was too difficult for him. He turned to Olivia for help.

'The fact is, Mr. Pim,' said Olivia, with a friendly smile, 'that we are very glad to see you, and that you must forgive us for troubling you like this. By the way, do you know Lady Marden?'

Mr. Pim didn't. They bowed to each other.

'Now come and sit here next to me.' The bewildered Mr. Pim followed her to the sofa and sat down. 'That's right.'

Perhaps, thought Mr. Pim, Lady Marden was to give him a letter of introduction.

'Well, now,' Olivia went on, 'what has happened is this. You gave us rather a surprise this morning, and before we had time to realize what it all meant, you had gone.'

'A surprise, Mrs. Marden? Dear me, not an unpleasant one, I hope?'

'Well, rather a surprising one.'

Mr. Pim's apologies were cut short by George.

'Olivia, allow me a moment,' He drew a chair up on the other side of Mr. Pim, and began. 'Mr. Pim. You mentioned a man called Telworthy this morning. Now, my wife used to—well, no, not my wife. That is, I used to—well, anyhow, there are reasons—'

'I think we had better be perfectly frank, George.'

Mr. Pim, entirely out of his depth, gazed helplessly from one to the other. Before he could say anything, while his mouth was yet open to begin, an unexpected wave from Lady Marden entirely submerged him.

'I am sixty-five years of age, Mr. Pim,' said Lady Marden threateningly, 'and I can assure you that I have never had a moment's uneasiness from telling the truth.'

Mr. Pim floated to the surface, came round slowly and gasped 'Oh!' Then, having got his breath again, he said:

'I'm afraid that I am rather at sea. Did I leave anything unsaid in presenting my credentials to you this morning?'

'Oh, no, no,' they assured him hastily.

He looked up at the ceiling, rubbing his chin in the effort to collect his memories.

'This man Telworthy whom you mention,' he said slowly; 'I seem to remember the name.'

Olivia came to his rescue.

'Mr. Pim, you told us this morning of a man whom you had met on the boat, a man who had come down in the world, whom you had known in Sydney. A man called Telworthy.'

'Ah, yes, yes.' He nodded vigorously. 'Of course. I did say Telworthy, didn't I?' At ease on this point again, he turned with his kindly smile to Lady Marden. 'A most curious coincidence, Lady Marden. Poor man, poor man! Let me see, it must have been nearly eight years ago, when I was staying in Sydney, that I—'

'Just a moment,' said George, controlling his impatience with difficulty. 'The point is, are you quite sure his name was Telworthy?'

'Telworthy? Telworthy?' He looked from one to the other in bewilderment. 'Didn't I say Telworthy?' Again he gazed at the ceiling for help, and then, completely reassured, came back to them once more. 'Yes, that was it,' he announced with absolute conviction. 'Telworthy.' He shook his head and sighed. 'Poor fellow!'

'I'm going to be perfectly frank with you, Mr. Pim,' said Olivia, taking up the tale. 'I feel sure that I can trust you.'

'My dear!' from the alarmed George.

She waved aside his protest and went on: 'This man Telworthy whom you met is my husband.'

'Your husband?' Mr. Pim looked at George reproachfully for having so deceived him.

'My first husband. His death was announced six years ago; I had left him some time before that. Now there seems to be no doubt from your story that he was still alive. His record—the country he was living in—above all, the very unusual name, Telworthy.'

Mr. Pim beamed at Olivia as another memory came back to him.

'Telworthy, yes. Certainly a *most* peculiar name. I remember saying so at the time. But your first husband! Dear me! Dear me!'

'You understand, Mr. Pim,' put in George anxiously, 'that all this is in absolute confidence?'

'Of course, of course—Telworthy, yes, a most peculiar name.'

'Well, since he is my husband,' resumed Olivia, 'we naturally want to know something more about him.' She leant forward anxiously. 'Where is he now, for instance?'

Mr. Pim looked at her in astonishment. 'Where is he now?' he repeated.

'Yes.'

'Where is he now? But I told you. Surely I told you.'

Olivia shook her head.

'I told you what happened at Marseilles?'

'At Marseilles?' frowned George.

'Yes, yes, poor fellow, it was most unfortunate.' He turned towards Lady Marden. He was nearly forgetting that she had not heard the story yet. How stupid of him!

'You must understand, Lady Marden,' he began, 'that although I had met the poor fellow before in Australia—in Sydney, to be precise—I was never in any way intimate—'

George could control himself no longer. Thumping the table in front of him, he shouted: 'Where is he *now*, that's what we want to know.'

Mr. Pim stopped with a jerk, and looked at the ferocious man in alarm.

'Please, Mr. Pim!' implored Olivia.

Mr. Pim was still mystified. He had told them this morning. An hour later he had told the Trevors.

'But, surely, you remember the curious fatality at Marseilles?'

'Marseilles?' echoed George and his Aunt Julia.

But now Olivia knew. She stood up and looked at Mr. Pim, and it was evident that she was struggling with some emotion.

'Yes, yes,' he went on, 'the fish bone.'

'Fish bone?' they echoed again.

'A herring, I understand,' explained Mr. Pim sadly.

Olivia kept trying to speak, but the words would not come. At last she got out, 'You mean he's dead?'

'Dead? Of course, he is dead. Didn't I tell you?'

Hysterically her laughter pealed out. The more reproachfully Mr. Pim looked at her, the more she laughed.

'Oh, Mr. Pim!' she said, shaking her head weakly at him. 'Oh, you—' But she could not finish that sentence. After another spasm she gasped, 'Oh, what a husband to have!'

Lady Marden could not abide weakness; particularly weakness in her own sex, the stronger sex.

'Pull yourself together, Olivia,' she commanded sternly. 'This is so unhealthy for you.'

But Olivia still rocked.

'So he really is dead this time?' said Lady Marden.

'Oh, undoubtedly. A fish bone lodged in his throat.'

'Dead!' said George dramatically. He raised his eyes to Heaven.

There was no hope of Olivia recovering in that room. George's face, Aunt Julia's face, Mr. Pim's face, they all made it impossible. Weakly she held out her hand to the visitor.

'I think you must excuse me, Mr. Pim,' she stammered. 'I can never thank you enough.' She caught back a spasm and hurried on, 'A herring … There's something about a herring … Morality depends on such little things, doesn't it?' Then she caught sight of George's face again, shook her head weakly, gasped, 'Oh, George! You—' and with another peal of laughter felt her way out of the room.

Lady Marden sniffed contemptuously.

III

So Telworthy was dead after all! He had died at Marseilles, and Olivia had gone into hysterics over it, and George was raising his eyes to Heaven and returning thanks for the great happiness which had come to him.

Was this the way to receive so solemn a matter?

Well, let us be frank about it. Every second (we are told) a man dies. If the man is nothing to us, can we grieve; or, grieving, have any time for laughter? But, in any case, can we grieve for the man himself, when we are so assured that he has left this world for a better? Our grief can only be for those whose happiness on earth has been blighted by his departure. In Telworthy's case, whose happiness was that? None whom George knew; none whom Olivia knew. Why should they pay the tribute to Propriety of a momentarily solemn face? George, being a vassal in that court, will pay directly, we may be sure, but Olivia had more sense, more candour. She laughed hysterically at the comedy of it. Whom was she outraging?

Dead! George's first feeling was one of triumph that his faith in the Providence which was looking after his affairs was justified. Over and over again he had said to himself in dazed bewilderment, 'That this should be happening to *us*!' How right he had been! Such things did not happen 'to us.' All along he had felt the unreality of it. It was only a nightmare; it must be only a nightmare, else his faith was shattered. Now the nightmare was over. Nothing had happened to disturb his faith. Indeed, it stood the stronger now, so brilliantly had Providence come out of the ordeal.

But there were moments when George felt that he was a man of affairs, one of those cool, level-headed Englishmen who had carved for us our tribute of 'a nation of shopkeepers.' What would such a man do now? It was obvious. With a sigh of relief at his escape from all this orgy of emotions, he turned to Mr. Pim and said firmly, master in his house once more:

'Now, Mr. Pim, let us have this quite clear. You tell us definitely that the man Telworthy, Jacob Telworthy, is dead?'

Mr. Pim blinked his eyes, and focused them with a little trouble on his host.

'Telworthy—yes.' And then, with a note of complaint in the question, 'Didn't I say Telworthy? This man I was telling you about—'

'He's dead?' repeated George sternly.

'Yes, yes, certainly; he died at Marseilles.'

George turned with utter relief in his eyes to his Aunt Julia. 'Dead!' he confirmed, nodding at her. There was just a suggestion in his voice that that was what the Mardens were like, when put to it.

'A dispensation of Providence,' pronounced Lady Marden gravely. 'One can look at it in no other light.'

But one may question whether she was wholly grateful to Providence. She had never approved of George's marriage to Olivia, and it was charitable to assume that an all-wise Providence shared her views on this matter. Even if it were true that the departure of Olivia from Marden House was not sufficient compensation for the scandal it would bring on the Marden name, yet, taken in conjunction with the opportunity afforded to Aunt Julia of saying, 'Well, I always warned you,' it could be faced with equanimity. And now Providence seemed to have deserted her. Well, one must suppose that it knew best.

'Dead!' said George solemnly again, almost as if he were a church bell tolling.

How good the calm was after the storm! How happy now he was just to be alive, and to know that Olivia was still his—his for ever! He shuddered as he thought what a narrow escape he had had, and, shuddering, realized suddenly that all these terrible hours he had been through had been an absolutely needless torture, a mere wanton sport of Mr. Pim's! For Telworthy had been dead all the time! He looked at that unfortunate old gentleman with a growing sense of indignation.

'Really, Mr. Pim,' he said severely, 'I think you might have told us this before.'

Mr. Pim couldn't make it out. He had been convinced that he *had* told them. Certainly he had told the Trevors—all except the name of the poor fellow, which had temporarily slipped his memory—because he remembered Mrs. Trevor making some comment about the dangers of fish bones, and the best way of treating a case of choking. The Trevors had been very much interested in the story, just as the Mardens had been. It was the same story.

'But I—I did tell you!' he protested. 'I certainly—' and then he stopped. For he remembered that George had interrupted him with the letter, before the story was finished, and had conducted him out through the windows immediately afterwards; wherefore he corrected himself now and said, 'I—I *was* telling you. But—'

'If you had only told us the whole story at once,' George went on, with simple dignity, 'instead of in two instalments like this, you would have saved us all a good deal of anxiety.'

'But really!' palpitated Mr. Pim.

'I am sure Mr. Pim meant well, George,' said Lady Marden, summing the case up judicially, 'but it seems a pity he couldn't have said it all before. If the man was dead, *why* try to hush it up?'

'Really, Lady Marden, I—I assure you—'

George stood up and gave Mr. Pim his friendly, charming smile. 'Well, well,' he said, forgiving the culprit whole-heartedly, 'I am very much obliged to you for having come down to us this afternoon. It was most good of you.' He held out his hand and, as Mr. Pim took it, tolled once more 'Dead!' Then with a solemn face he paid his tribute to Propriety. '*De mortuis*—and so forth,' he said reverently, 'but the situation would have been an impossible one had he lived. Good-bye, Mr. Pim.'

Mr. Pim was still clutching George's hand, the one solid thing in a world of shadows. He had said good-bye to that hand once already this morning; had said it and gone away, leaving his story, so it seemed, unfinished. What had happened to his story now? They were confusing him dreadfully; they were hurrying him. The Trevors had given him more time. At lunch he had told the story at his leisure—all except the man's name. Telworthy! Now it came back to him.

Lady Marden, appealed to by George's eye, held out her hand.

'Good-bye, Mr. Pim,' she said, a trifle severely.

Mr. Pim let George's hand go and clutched at Lady Marden's.

'I am sure, Lady Marden,' he began, 'if I had only known—'

'That's all right, Mr. Pim,' beamed George. 'Got your hat? That's right. You must let us drive you back to the Trevors. I expect the trap will be waiting. I like horses in the country. Hope you agree with me.'

'Thank you, thank you, yes, but I am not going back to the Trevors. And I shall like the little walk.'

'The Brymers, what? Well, just as you please. It's no trouble, you know.'

'No, no, I shall like the little walk. Good-bye, Lady Marden.'

He gave her a dignified little bow, and followed George to the windows. But at the windows he stopped for a moment, gazed up at the sky, and murmured to himself, 'Telworthy, yes. I *think* that was the name.'

And so out of Marden House again.

IV

The Head of the Mardens, the special *protégé* of Providence, our George, came back to his Aunt Julia in the best of good spirits. Forgetting in his excitement the most elementary rules of hygiene, he kissed her loudly and, before she had recovered, patted her heavily on the back in the manner of one administering first-aid.

'Really, George,' she protested, 'it was not I who swallowed the fish bone.'

'What?' He threw his head back and laughed heartily. 'Well done, Aunt Julia!' Stretching himself luxuriously he cried, 'Ah, but this is wonderful news! It is almost worth going through what I have gone through to feel as I feel now.'

'Quite so,' she said dryly. She looked at him with a grim smile. 'You realize, of course, that you are not married to Olivia?'

He turned to her vacantly, repeating, 'Not married?'

'Naturally, if her first husband only died a few days ago at Marseilles.'

His jaw dropped. No, he wasn't married to Olivia. Good heavens!

'Not that it matters,' went on his aunt. 'You can easily get married again. Quietly. Nobody need know.'

'Yes.' Then another thought came to him. 'So that all these years we have been—er—yes.'

'Who's going to know?'

'Yes, that's true. And in perfect innocence. Still—er—yes.'

For the fact remained that even now he was not, had never been, married to Olivia. Even if Mr. Pim had told his story in one instalment, there would have been the fact. Obviously there was nothing for it now but to get married again as quickly as possible—thank Heaven that his duty was absolutely clear this time; Heaven be thanked also that this time duty coincided with desire—but still the fact remained, a cloud in the glorious blue which had been vouchsafed to him so suddenly. They had lived together for five years unmarried!

For, as he had protested truly to Olivia, he did not think only of the scandal. There need be no scandal now, yet he was still distressed. Right or wrong, his moral standard was there, and he lived up to it. No man can do more. As he would have put it, they had 'sinned innocently', nor would he have agreed that if it were done innocently it could not be a sin. They had done wrong; as far as the wrong could be righted, they would put it right; and then, safely married, they would begin again, a world of happiness at their feet. But still—they had done wrong.

'I should suggest a registry office in London,' said Lady Marden, getting back to business.

'A registry office, Aunt Julia?' he questioned, surprised.

'Easier. Quicker. Less talk.'

'Y—yes.'

But then they would never have been married in Church! And yet Aunt Julia was right—there were difficulties in the way of a church service ... and, after all, according to the law of the land a registry office was enough ... and for Olivia's sake (this was a good thought)—for Olivia's sake, it must be done as quietly as possible ... still, he would have preferred a church. Perhaps if they went into a church together *after* the registry office, just to solemnize the proceedings a bit; there were always services going on in the London churches—they could sit for a moment in the Abbey ...

He nodded happily to himself. Yes, that was what they would do.

'A registry office, yes,' he agreed cheerfully.

'Better go up to town this afternoon. Can't do it too quickly.'

'Yes, yes.' He became the man of affairs again. 'We can stay at an hotel—Baker's—I'll send them a telegram—'

'George!' exclaimed Aunt Julia in amazement.

'What?'

'*You* will stay at your club.'

Once again he remembered that he was not married to Olivia.

'Quite so, Aunt Julia,' he agreed hastily.

'Better take your solicitor with you to be on the safe side.'

George looked at her in surprise. Was so much chaperonage really necessary?

'To the registry office, I mean,' she explained.

'Oh yes. Yes, undoubtedly.'

He sank into thought. And as he thought, his face softened, and there was a tender look in his eyes, very winning, a tender smile at the corners of his mouth. Olivia was his, undisputed. A day or two of unpleasantness, and then his for ever! That was the one great fact in the world.

'Well, I must be getting along, George,' interrupted Lady Marden. 'Say good-bye to Olivia for me. And those children? Of course, you won't allow this absurd love-business between them to come to anything?'

George had forgotten them. But he reassured Aunt Julia on the point at once. Most certainly he would not allow it to go on.

'That's right. And get Olivia out more. I don't like these hysterics; it's all so unhealthy. You want to be firmer with her, George.'

'Yes, yes,' said George firmly. But just then he only wanted to be alone with her, with his beautiful Olivia. 'Yes, yes, you're quite right, Aunt Julia.' He walked with her to the door, answering her questions absently. His mind was with Olivia. His now for ever.

Chapter Twelve

Mrs. Telworthy Receives a Proposal

I

But the absurd love-business was still going on between those two children.

'Kiss me,' commanded Dinah, as soon as they were away from the house. Brian kissed her. It was her official defiance, childish if you like, of George's authority. To their thinking he had betrayed Olivia. By that betrayal they were absolved of their pledge to him. So Brian kissed her. It was not a question now of 'uncles or no uncles.' Dinah felt that henceforward she had no uncle. There remained only her guardian, George Marden. He might forbid the marriage until she were twenty-one; so much perhaps the Law allowed him; but meanwhile she owed him no respect, no love, no duty.

'I suppose the fact is,' said Brian, 'he's never really been in love with her at all, not what *we* call being in love.'

'I think he was when he was proposing to her, you know. He was a bit off his food about then. I remember wondering what was the matter with him. Of course, as soon as I saw them together—' She broke off, and added, 'Oh yes, he was, Brian, awfully. Not like *us*, of course, but still, very, very—Brian,' she turned to him seriously, 'it *is* possible isn't it, to go on being in love with one another always?'

Brian swore that it was. In their case, not only possible, but inevitable.

'Of course, you were bound to say that,' she said wistfully. 'Then why did you ask me?'

'Oh well, I had to.'

'What's the matter, darling?'

'I don't know. Nothing. Let's sit down.' She curled herself up on the grass, and Brian lay beside her, selecting and nibbling the more succulent stalks.

'That's very dangerous,' she said, after watching him in silence. 'I know a man—at least, I didn't know him, but it really happened—and he got all sorts of horrible things inside him by doing that. Eggs and things which grew up.'

'I expect he did it on Sunday,' said Brian lazily, 'when he ought to have been in church. It wouldn't happen to a really good man like me.'

'What little you know about me really,' she went on. 'I'm horrid sometimes ... And selfish. Oh, selfish!'

'So am I.'

'Men are always supposed to be, aren't they? But it's a different sort of selfish ... Wasn't it awful what I said to Olivia about nothing ever happening here? Only a beast would have said that.'

'She understood,' said Brian. 'And I shall understand.'

'Will you?' She looked at him thoughtfully. 'I believe you will. I think you're the most understanding man I've ever met.'

This was love only. He acknowledged it with a smile. But was he understanding? Did he understand George, for instance?

Suppose he, Brian, had to choose between Dinah and his art? Impossible! But just suppose? Suppose George were now choosing between Olivia and his God? It was not good enough merely to say that it was a false god. His own art might be false art; certainly was in George's eyes. The point was that George believed in his God. Then what could he do but fight for Him? Brian's God was not as George's; it was, for instance, a betrayal of Brian's God to paint a picture in which he did not believe. Would Brian so betray Him for Dinah's sake? It was horrible.

'What's the matter, darling?'

'Matter?' he asked vacantly.

'You're frowning so.' She put a cool hand on his forehead, and smoothed out the wrinkles. 'You're spoiling the face I love.'

He laughed and explained. 'I was thinking of George.'

'Oh, well!'

'No, not like that, Dinah.' He became very busy with the grass, pulling it up and examining it minutely. 'I was thinking perhaps I—I hadn't been—quite fair to him.'

'Brian!' Indignant surprise from Dinah.

'Well, I mean he's all wrong, of course—'

'I should think so!'

'But even if you're wrong ... there's a sort of right way of being wrong. ... I mean, if you do think like that, and I suppose he does—' He put a piece of grass in his mouth and added, unexpectedly, 'Or am I only being a prig?'

'You could make out anything to be right like that.'

Brian sighed. 'Yes, I suppose you could.'

'And why should you be fair to him; he wasn't fair to you.'

'No, but then I never mind that.'

'Well, I don't suppose he minds what *you* think.' She leant over and kissed his hand. 'Darling, that sounds beastly, but you know what I mean.'

'Of course. And you're quite right. He doesn't mind. But that's no reason for—' he left it unfinished, and after a little silence said solemnly. 'Do you know, Dinah, that there are weak unmanly moments in my life—this is a confession, so make a note of it—weak unmanly moments when I tell myself that it is just possible I am *not* invariably right about everything.'

'I expect you're right about that, anyway,' smiled Dinah.

'Thank you. In fact, at this moment I am only certain about one thing.'

'Which is—?'

He held out his hands to her.

'That I love you, I love you, I love you.'

Dinah felt suddenly that George didn't really matter very much.

II

Olivia, not quite knowing how, found her way up to her bedroom and collapsed into a chair. It was difficult to get full control of herself. At one moment she would be calm, at the next a sudden remembrance of George's Heaven-be-thanked face, of Mr. Pim's bewilderment, of Lady Marden's mixed reception of the good news, would set her off again. 'It isn't funny, it isn't funny, it's very serious,' she would say to herself, biting her lower lip in a determined effort not to laugh, and then, when that was useless: 'Anyhow, it isn't *really* funny; it's only like sitting down on your hat.' But as a relief from tragedy, even from mere drabness, the sight of another sitting on his hat is exquisitely funny, coming with an irresistible force to the subtlest sense of humour.

It was the sight of her face in the glass which turned her thoughts at last to the serious business of life. 'Oh, my dear, you *are* plain; no wonder he wanted to get rid of you,' she murmured, and proceeded to make herself more worth keeping. A powder-puff is a devastating weapon in the hands of a woman. You or I, my dear sir, would powder our noses and merely look foolish. A woman powders her soul. 'Now I am all right,' she says, returning the puff, and looks it, and we worship her. 'Now, I am all wrong,' we should say with equal conviction, and look it, and be laughed at. For there is no merit in the actual powder.

Our masculine noses (to mention them again) get along quite comfortably without it.

Olivia, reassured about herself, went to the window. There was Mr. Pim! She stood against the curtains watching George, the perfect host, speed him from Marden House. 'Good-bye, Mr. Pim, you will never come into our lives again. But do I thank you for coming into them this once, or don't I?'

She sat down to think it out. How did she stand with George now? What difference to their relations did the discoveries of this afternoon make?

She knew now the whole truth about him. But was it the whole truth? Is it the whole truth about a man to say that he is a coward, because in one crisis he behaves like a coward? Our life is not made up of crises. For every one of us there is a test too severe; we can only pray that we shall not be called upon to meet it or, meeting it, may fight and lose alone. Most of us are fortunate; we can go on from year to year, hiding the truth about ourselves from our friends; perhaps we are more fortunate still in that the truth about our friends remains hidden from us—if it be the truth. But to some the test comes in the presence of those whom they love the most; their souls are bared to their friends, who turn away, shrinking. Yet is it the real man whom we have seen, or that unworthy substitute who is waiting his chance with all of us?

'But that won't do,' said Olivia to herself. 'It was not an unexpected George who showed himself this afternoon; it was the real George, the George I married.'

There was one part of her crying out that she was hurt, that her life would never be the same again; there was another part of her insisting that she was only hurt if she allowed herself to be hurt, and that life was always the same again. It rested with her to make the best or the worst of it. Which was she going to do?

How few of us can deny ourselves a grievance! We are prepared to be generous, none more so. In a day, in an hour, even now at this moment we will forgive, we will welcome the offender again to our bosom. But there is one inexorable condition. It must be quite clear to him that he *is* the offender. If we failed to have our grievance, he would never realize our magnanimity. He would think that we had nothing to forgive; that his offence was not, or had passed unnoticed; even—horrible thought—that the offence was ours, and that it was he who was the magnanimous one, greeting us again without a word of reproach. So, we tell ourselves, it would not be right to give up our grievance. He must see plainly that he has hurt us, before the reconciling embrace. We forgive, he is forgiven—there must be no misunderstanding about our attitudes. The bent head is his; the outstretched reassuring hand is ours.

Olivia saw that this must be so, even with a smile at herself for seeing it. 'Ah, my dear, thank Heaven you are my wife again! Now we can be happy'—George must not get off as lightly as that. Besides—and here the smile became more pronounced— she was not his wife again. She was Mrs. Telworthy.

She was not fond of grievances, she never sulked, she would not show a hurt reproachful face to George. But she was determined now to take charge. It had been George's morning; the first part of the afternoon had been his; the rest of the day, the next few days, would be hers. It was to be she now who would say what was to be done or what was not to be done. The engagement between Brian and Dinah should be recognized; the curtains—now the smile was very mischievous—yes, the curtains should be hung.

She told herself now that she was not hurt. George had been George, but he loved her. That moment, just before Mr. Pim came in, when their eyes met, and she called to him, called to him with her whole heart, was the proof of his love. He had been coming to her. In spite of all that was against her—laws, habits, traditions, the gods whom he had set up, all tugging him the other way—she had been winning. His despairing cry,

'I want to do what's right,' had been wrung from him by her eyes. Another moment, and he would have come to her, right or wrong. What higher tribute could he pay her?

She looked at herself in the glass again, smiled at it, and then, the smile still on her lips, walked leisurely down the stairs. What a comedy life was, when once you had realized that you couldn't play it as tragedy. The laugh trembled on her mouth as she thought again of those last moments with Mr. Pim, but she tucked it firmly away. Now then, George.

III

George jumped up as Olivia came into the room, and bore down upon her with outstretched hands.

'Olivia!' he cried.

Just for a moment she faltered, and then, with a magnificent gesture, she motioned him back.

'Mrs. Telworthy,' she said proudly. No actress on the stage, she felt, could have done it with a more superb air.

His surprise was ludicrous.

'I—I don't understand,' he stammered.

She had to laugh then, but she did it very naturally and pleasantly, moving across to the sofa and inviting him with a look to come too.

'Poor George!' she said. 'Did I frighten you rather?'

'You're so strange to-day,' he protested, sitting down next to her and trying to take her hands. 'I don't understand you. You're not like the Olivia I know.'

'Perhaps you don't know me very well after all.'

'Oh, that's nonsense, old girl. You're just my Olivia.'

She shot a smile at him and said: 'And yet it seemed as though I were somebody else's Olivia half an hour ago.'

He moved uncomfortably at that.

'Don't let's talk about it,' he said hurriedly. 'It doesn't bear thinking about.'

'Ah, no!' sighed Olivia, eyes to Heaven, and then quickly from Heaven to George, and back to Heaven again.

'Well, thank God that's over. And now we can get married again quietly, and nobody will be any the wiser.'

She turned an innocent face to him. 'Married again?' she repeated, apparently not understanding.

'Yes, dear. As you—er—said just now'—he ventured an amused laugh, but only achieved the skeleton of it—'you are Mrs. Telworthy, just for the moment.' He patted her hand, and went on soothingly, 'But we can soon put that right. My idea,' he went on, elbowing Aunt Julia out of it, 'was to go up this evening and make arrangements, and if you come up to-morrow afternoon, if we can manage it by then, we could get quietly married at a registry office, and—er—nobody any the wiser.'

He waited for her approval of his extraordinary grip on the situation. She nodded at him.

'Yes, I see. You want me to marry you at a registry office to-morrow?'

'Yes, if we can manage it by then. I don't know how long these things take, but I should imagine—my solicitor would know, of course—I dare say I could see him to-night—'

He hurried on, hoping to keep Olivia's attention off the dangerous words—'registry office.' He had had his own qualms of conscience about this, but they were now subdued. He was persuaded—well, almost persuaded—that his duty as a Christian summoned him to a registry office rather than a church, for the reason that the registry office offered speedier facilities for marriage; well, he supposed they did, but his solicitor would know about that; and, surely the one important thing for both of them was to get married as quickly as possible. True, a registry office was less public than a church, but that was not the point. The point was—well, anyhow, he did not want to argue it with Olivia, who was sometimes obtuse about these things, adorable though she was in other respects.

However, this afternoon Olivia was not arguing about such details as registry offices. She smiled to herself as she listened, understanding him so clearly, but she was challenging the main idea now. To his great relief she agreed carelessly to all that he said; that was all right. But—

'But what?' he asked.

'Well, if you want to marry me to-morrow, oughtn't you to propose to me first?'

He looked at her in amazement. What on earth did she mean.

'It is usual, isn't it,' she went on calmly, 'to propose to a person before you marry her? And'—another mischievous little smile was lurking—'we want to do the usual thing, don't we?'

Yes, George always wanted to do the usual thing, but he had lost his bearings for the moment. Seeing this, Olivia explained to him very simply just where he was.

'You see, dear, you're George Marden, and I'm Olivia Telworthy, and you are—well, you're attracted by me. You think I would make you a good wife, and you want to marry me to-morrow at a registry office. Well, then'—she held up an admonishing forefinger—'naturally you propose to me first, and tell me how much you are attracted by me, and what a good wife you think I shall make, and how badly you want to marry me.'

George followed this with open mouth. Gradually, as he began to understand, the mouth went up at the corners, intelligence gleamed in the eyes. There was a broad smile on his face by the time she had finished.

'The baby!' He threw his head back and laughed heartily. Then, humorously soothing, 'Did she want to be proposed to all over again?'

'Well, she did rather,' said Olivia, enjoying quite a different joke.

George stood up, still chuckling.

'She shall, then.'

It was no doubt merely the accident of birth which had deprived the stage of a great actor in George. To a man of his position, the arts were just a relaxation for which as yet he had had no opportunity. George was a busy man. He had not the time on his hands which these actor fellows and writing fellows had. Granted the time, the achievements of the popular favourites are within the reach of all of us; those of us, at any rate, who have had the advantage of a public-school education. To doubt this is to concede too much to these artist fellows.

Light-heartedly, then, he sketched his idea of the lover proposing.

'Mrs. Telworthy,' he began, hand on heart, 'I have long admired you in silence, and the time has now come to put my admiration into words.' Excellent! There should have been an audience. Now how should he go on? 'Er—er—'

'Into words,' Olivia reminded him.

'Er—'

She continued to wait patiently. Then, with the idea of helping him, she looked bashfully away, and murmured, 'Oh, Mr. Marden!'

That gave him his cue. 'May I call you Olivia?' he asked sternly.

'Yes, George.'

He took her hand.

'Olivia—I—er—h'r'm'—' he announced, and was just getting into the swing of it, when the thoughtless woman broke in:

'I don't want to interrupt, but oughtn't you to be on your knees? It is—usual, I believe. If one of the servants came in, you could say that you were looking for my scissors.'

He threw at her the indignant look of the painter interrupted in the middle of his most delicate brush- work.

'Really, Olivia,' he protested, 'you must allow me to manage my own proposal in my own way.'

'I'm sorry. Do go on.'

'Well, then—er—' No, it was no good. A masterpiece had been ruined. 'Confound it, Olivia, I love you,' he burst out. 'Will you marry me?'

It had come at last, the proposal for which she had been waiting. She bent her head in acknowledgment of it.

'Thank you, George,' she said quietly. 'I will think it over.'

George laughed admiringly. Olivia, it seemed, was a bit of an actress, too. But the play-acting had gone on long enough. They must get back to business.

'Silly girl,' he smiled, and touched her cheek. 'Well, then, to-morrow morning. No wedding-cake, I'm afraid, old girl,' he laughed again. 'But we'll go and have a good lunch somewhere.'

She looked up at him and repeated firmly: 'I will think it over, George.'

'Well, give us a kiss while you're thinking,' he said, half annoyed at her elaboration of the joke, half amused by it. He bent down to her.

'I'm afraid you mustn't kiss me until we are actually engaged,' she explained, turning her face away.

For the first time something in her manner disturbed him. Was it possible that—No, impossible. He laughed awkwardly, to reassure himself.

'Oh, we needn't take it as seriously as all that.'

'But a woman must take a proposal seriously,' she said, still quite calm, quite matter-of-fact.

'What do you mean?' He was now really alarmed.

'Well, I mean that the whole question—as I heard somebody say once—demands much more anxious thought than either of

161

us has given it.' She glanced at him to see if he was recognizing his own words, and went on: 'These hasty marriages—'

'Hasty!' he put in sarcastically.

'Well, you've only just proposed to me, and you want to marry me to-morrow.'

Olivia was now merely being absurd. It was his duty to tell her so.

'You know, you're talking perfect nonsense,' he said. 'You know quite well that our case is utterly different from'—he hesitated—'from any other,' he ended lamely.

Olivia smiled to herself. Yes, he *had* recognized his own words. He remembered the occasion of them.

'All the same,' she answered, 'one has to ask oneself questions. With a young girl like'—she pulled herself up, just as he had done—'well, with a young girl,' she corrected herself, 'love may well seem to be all that matters. But with a woman of my age it is different. When a man proposes to me I have to ask myself if he can afford to support a wife.'

'Fortunately, that is a question which you can very easily answer for yourself,' he said coldly. He didn't know what she was talking about.

'Well, but I have been hearing rather bad reports lately. What with—er—taxes always going up, and—er—rents always going down, some of our landowners are getting into rather straitened circumstances. At least,' she added, wishing to be fair, 'that's what I have been told.'

'I don't know what you're talking about,' he growled. But he did know now.

She looked at him in surprise. 'Isn't it true?' she asked. 'Of course I may have been misinformed.' He had nothing to say and she went on, 'I heard of a case only this morning—a landowner who always seemed to be very comfortably off, but who couldn't afford an allowance for his favourite niece when she wanted to get married.' She gave a little sigh for the distressing situation, and proceeded to draw the moral. 'It made me think,' she said gravely, 'that one oughtn't to judge by appearances.'

George was now thoroughly annoyed. It was damnably unfair to make this use of his few harmless remarks of the morning. It was well known that when a man said that he couldn't afford this, that or the other, all he meant was that— well, he had another use for his money. And why not?

'You know perfectly well that I can support a wife as my wife should be supported,' he said with dignity.

Her brow cleared. She turned to him, all smiles.

'Oh, I'm so glad, dear. Then your income—you aren't *really* getting anxious?'

He reminded her stiffly that she knew quite well what his income was, and what, presumably, it would remain.

'Then that's all right,' she said with relief. 'We needn't think about that any more.'

She pushed down the first finger of her left hand, and passed on to the second finger. 'Well, now there's another thing to be considered.'

He broke away from her at that, and stalked over to his desk, making indignant noises. What on earth was she up to?

He knew, but he would not confess it to himself. To admit that she was paying him back for his betrayal of her that afternoon was to admit that he had betrayed her. Already he was ashamed of himself, yet refused to allow it. He had a hundred excuses for himself, where no excuses were necessary, and knew in his heart that not one of the hundred would do. He had acted as his conscience had urged him, yet remained conscience-stricken.

'I can't make out what you're up to,' he muttered uneasily. 'Don't you *want* to get married? Don't you want to—er—legalize this extraordinary situation in which we are placed?'

She answered seriously. 'I want to be sure that I am going to be happy.' And then with a sudden fall from gravity, 'I can't just jump at the very first offer I have had since my husband died, without considering the whole question very carefully.'

'I'm under consideration, eh?'

'Every suitor is.'

So he was a suitor again! Masters of the House, Lords in our Castles, Keepers of the Purse, we were all suitors once, although we have forgotten it, conveniently enough, now. There was a day when we were on our knees, begging the proud beauty to turn to us, to throw us one kind word, one little smile. Her lightest wish was law to us. Edelweiss or Emeralds, she breathed the desire and we were off in pursuit. Look at us now! Listen to us now! What, this pompous fellow ever a suitor? 'I am sorry, my dear, but I have said my last word on the subject.' And once, soul bared before her, he was at her feet, praying her not to say that last word which would send him into the darkness. No wonder that he has forgotten it now; no wonder that she will remember ever.

He was a suitor again. Gone was the lordship, the authority, the word of command; gone the ease and mastery, companions of the knowledge that one belongs—good heavens, yes—to the superior sex. The woman has her hour, and Olivia's hour was come again.

'Go on,' he said gruffly.

She went on.

'Well, then there's your niece. You have a niece who lives with you. Of course, Dinah is a delightful girl, but one doesn't like marrying into a household in which there is another grown-up woman.' She looked up at him as if an idea had suddenly occurred to her. 'But perhaps she will be getting married herself soon?'

'I see no prospect of it,' announced George.

There was a moment's silence.

'I think,' said Olivia gently, 'it would make it much easier if she did.'

She did not look at him, but she could feel the comprehension of it creeping over his face, a comprehension which left him speechless.

'Much easier,' she repeated.

So that was it! It was not enough that he should fall on his knees to her again; not enough that he should pay—against all precedent, a second time—formal homage to her sovereignty. Something more material was required of him. She was issuing terms.

'Is this a threat, Olivia?' he demanded, in the voice which had convicted many a vagrant of impiety after a night in the open. 'Are you telling me that if I do not allow young Strange to marry Dinah, you will not marry me?'

Put like that, can we be surprised that Olivia quailed before it?

'A threat? Oh no, George.'

'Then what does it mean?'

'Well, I was just wondering if you loved me as much as— well, as much as Brian loves Dinah.'

Confound that fellow Strange! Why did she want to drag him into it.

In answer to his thoughts she let the fellow go and asked instead: 'You *do* love me, George?'

Ah, he could answer now.

'You know I do, old girl,' he said earnestly.

'You're not just attracted by my pretty face?' Innocently she added, 'Is it a pretty face?'

Ah, that too he could answer. From his whole heart he cried, 'It's an adorable one, my darling.'

Again he tried to kiss it, but, as if not noticing his movement, she turned away.

'How can I be sure,' she wondered, 'that it is not *only* my face which makes you think that you care for me? Love,' she mused 'which only rests upon a mere outward attraction cannot lead to any lasting happiness.' She sighed, and added a little unkindly, 'As one of our thinkers has observed.'

Damnably unfair! As if anything which middle-age said to youth ought to be used in evidence against middle-age! Why, it would make life impossible. Education and religion would be handicapped out of existence.

'What's come over you, Olivia?' he asked. 'I don't understand what you're driving at.' Feebly he added, 'Why should you doubt my love?'

Ah, why? He knew. She knew that he knew. Hurriedly he went on, lest she should take advantage of that unlucky question, 'You can't pretend that we haven't been happy together. I've been a good pal to you, eh? We—we suit each other, old girl.'

'Do we?'

'Of course we do,' he said persuasively.

'I wonder. When two people of our age think of getting married, one wants to be very sure that there is real community of ideas between them. Whether it is a comparatively trivial matter, like'—she hesitated, trying to think of an illustration for her meaning and glanced round the room for inspiration—'well, like the right colour for a curtain,' she threw out innocently, 'or whether it is some very much more serious question of conduct which arises, one wants to feel that there is some chance of agreement between husband and wife.'

The right colour for a curtain! Was that to be another of the terms?

'We love each other, old girl,' he pleaded. What did colours for curtains matter, compared with the great fact that they loved each other? Colours for curtains were nothing; particularly when all the husband had to say was: 'I won't have them in my house,' and all the wife had to say was 'Very well, George!' Now love—

'We love each other now, perhaps,' said Olivia. 'But what shall we be like in five years' time? Supposing that, after we had been married five years, we found ourselves estranged from each other upon such questions as'—she hesitated again, evidently trying to think of possible questions over which they might be estranged in five years' time—'well, such questions as Dinah's future, or the decorations of the drawing-room; even over the advice to give to a friend who had innocently contracted a bigamous marriage. How bitterly then we should regret our hasty plunge into a matrimony which was no true partnership, whether of tastes, or of ideas, or even of—consciences.' She leant back and sighed to Heaven 'Ah me!' It was a long-worded speech to have made, and she hoped that George would appreciate it.

No doubt if he had heard it properly, he would have liked it very much. But as it happened, a brilliant idea had just come to him, which prevented him from following it closely. For he was now about to turn the tables on her.

'Unfortunately for your argument, Olivia,' he said, in a voice which foreshadowed his approaching triumph, 'I can answer you out of your own mouth.'

She looked at him in alarm.

'You seem to have forgotten,' he went on, 'what you said this morning in the case of young Strange.'

'George!' she said reproachfully. 'Is it fair to drag up what was said this morning?'

He reminded her—she had apparently forgotten—that she was the one to begin it.

'I?' she asked in innocent surprise.

He assured her that it was the fact.

'Well, and what did I say this morning?'

'You said that it was quite enough that Strange was a gentleman and in love with Dinah for me to let them marry each other.'

'But *is* that enough?' she asked with interest.

'You said so!' The triumph rang out clearly now.

'Well, if you think so, I—perhaps you're right.' The meekest of wives was speaking.

'Aha, my dear!' he crowed. 'You see!' As he had always said, no woman could stand up against a man in argument for long.

'Then do you think it's enough?'

'Well—obviously—'

She went to him then, holding out her arms.

'My darling one! Then we can have a double wedding. How lovely!'

'A *double* one?' he said frowning.

'Of course; you and me, Brian and Dinah.'

Quite suddenly George felt that there must be a flaw in his brilliant idea. He stood gaping at her.

'You and me,' she murmured again, flipping up two fingers of the right hand, 'Brian and Dinah,' and up went two fingers of the left hand.

George was now quite certain that there was either a flaw, or else that he had failed to handle it properly. However, there was only one line to take now.

'Now, look here, Olivia,' he said firmly, 'understand once and for all that I am not to be blackmailed into giving my consent to Dinah's engagement. Neither blackmailed nor tricked. Our marriage'—he emphasized it with a sweeping gesture of the hand—'has nothing whatever to do with Dinah's.'

'No, dear,' said Olivia. 'I quite understand. They may take place about the same time, but they have nothing to do with each other.'

George observed coldly that he saw no prospect of Dinah's marriage taking place for many years.

'Yes, dear,' she agreed. 'That was what I said.'

'What you said?' he asked, amazed.

She nodded. His mouth was just open to explain to her what she had said when the explanation came to him. He closed it and stood looking at her, almost in horror. Could she really mean that? But even if she meant it in theory, in practice it was absolutely impossible. She would soon see that.

'We had better have this perfectly clear, Olivia. You apparently insist on treating my—er—proposal as serious.'

'But wasn't it serious? George,' she added wickedly, 'were you trifling with me?'

'You know quite well what I mean.' He spoke with dignity. 'You treat it as an ordinary proposal from a man to a woman who have been no more than acquaintances before. Very well, then. Will you tell me what you mean to do if you decide—er—not to marry me? You do not suggest that we should go on living together unmarried?'

It was her first chance of being shocked.

'Of *course* not, George!' she said indignantly. 'What would the County—I mean Heaven—I mean the Law—I mean, of *course* not! Besides,' she smiled, 'it's so unnecessary. If I decide to accept you, of course I shall marry you.'

'Quite so. But if you—er—decide to refuse me? What will you do then?'

Now he had got her. It was all very well for her to talk as she had talked, but when it came to the point, she would find that she had no choice in the matter. She would have to marry him; to pretend anything else was bluff.

'What will you do then?' he repeated.

'Nothing,' said Olivia calmly.

'Meaning by that?'

'Just that, George. I shall stay here just as before. I like this house. It wants a little redecorating, perhaps, but I do like it, George.' She looked round at the room, at the view from the windows, with a happy sigh. 'Yes, I shall be quite all right here,' she announced.

'I see. So you will continue to live down here in spite of what you said just now, about the immorality of it?' Surely she couldn't mean that!

She looked at him in surprise for a moment, and then leant forward to argue it out.

'But there's nothing immoral in a widow living alone in a big country house,' she assured him, 'with perhaps the niece of a friend staying with her, just to keep her company.'

'And what shall *I* be doing,' he asked, layers of sarcasm in his voice, 'when you've so kindly taken possession of my house for me?'

'I don't know, George. Travelling, I expect.' Then an idea occurred to her. 'You could come down sometimes with a chaperon,' she said brightly. 'I suppose there would be nothing wrong in that.'

He could stutter out no more than an indignant 'Thank you.' She waved it airily away, only too glad to have been of any help to him.

'And what if I refuse to be turned out of my house?' he demanded.

'Then, seeing that we can't both be in it, it looks as though you would have to turn *me* out.' Carelessly she added: 'I suppose there are legal ways of doing these things. You would have to consult your solicitor again.'

'Legal ways?' repeated the amazed George.

'Well, you couldn't *throw* me out, could you?'

No, he couldn't throw her out. Force is an effective weapon, only so long as it is kept in reserve, so long, that is to say, as it is used morally, not physically. 'Do this, or I'll make you,' says the big man to the little man, the big nation to the little nation, in the hope that the threat will be sufficient having the authority of Force behind it. But if the authority is not recognized, Force itself can do nothing. 'All right, make me,' says the little man to the big man, and the big man is powerless.

No, George could not make Olivia leave his house; he could not make her marry him. She ought to have recognized that he was the stronger; that, in addition, he had all the majesty of the

Law behind him; and, recognizing these things, she should have obeyed him meekly. But, as she would not recognize them, what could he do?

'You'll have to get an injunction against me,' she suggested cheerfully, 'or prosecute me for trespass, or something. Your solicitor will know. It would make an awfully unusual case, wouldn't it?' she went on in an interested voice. 'The papers would be full of it.'

The papers! An unusual case! George shuddered. It would be an absolutely impossible case.

Leaning back, her eyes closed, Olivia murmured in the monotonous voice of the newspaper-seller, a few possible headlines.

'Widow of well-known ex-convict takes possession of J.P.'s house! Popular country gentleman denied entrance to own home! Doomed to travel!'

George turned on her furiously.

'I've had enough of this,' he shouted. 'Do you mean all this nonsense?'

'I do mean, George,' she answered seriously, 'that I am in no hurry to go up to London and get married. I love the country just now; and, after this morning'—she gave a little sigh—'I am rather tired of husbands.'

'I've never heard so much damned nonsense in all my life,' exclaimed one of the husbands. He strode to the door. 'I will leave you to come to your senses.' A violent slam announced that he had left her.

As soon as he was gone Olivia jumped up to her feet, blew a loving kiss after him, and then, her face all triumphant smiles, stretched out her arms to her curtains. The dear things were really going up now!

Chapter Thirteen

Return of Mr. Pim

I

The door of the library swung open and George strode in. He hurried across to the nearest window, and opened it yet wider; then to the next window—it was shut—Good God! wasn't a man allowed to have air in his own house?—and so round the walls, until the pleasant July afternoon could step into the room from all three sides at once, bringing the peace of the lawns with it. The door of the library remained open—Good God! wasn't a man allowed to have privacy in his own house? He kicked it shut, damning it for the noise it made.

Here was a pretty state of things! Socialism! Revolution! Anarchy! His own women-folk, Olivia, Dinah, both defying him. It would be his servants next. He would give Anne an order and she would refuse to obey it. Anarchy!

He filled his pipe, stuffing in the tobacco furiously, and then, finding no matches in his pocket, rang the bell. Nothing happened. The revolution had begun. Second after second went by; still no Anne. Probably singing 'The Red Flag' somewhere. Mutiny, that's what it was. Rank mutiny. Take it in hand at once—the only way. He strode to the door ... and pulled himself up with a jerk. It was opening.

'Yes, sir?' said Anne, quiet, respectful, obedient.

'I want some matches. There never seems to be any. There ought to be plenty of boxes everywhere, in every room.'

Anne's eyes travelled in one rapid movement from the box on the chimney-piece to the box on the table, and from the box on the table to the box on the desk. And so back to the floor. 'Yes, sir,' she said apologetically, and glided out after a fourth box. In an incredibly short time she was back, the fourth box on a salver, and George, who realized now that it was the fourth box, was thanking her awkwardly. The bend of her head indicated that it was a pleasure to do anything for so perfect a gentleman; it even seemed to suggest, in some subtle way, that to serve a master who was content with three boxes of matches would have given her no happiness at all. As George lit his pipe she glided to the door. One got the impression that she was just waiting there for the actual striking of the match, in order to make sure that a fifth box would not be necessary. The ignition being satisfactory, she glided out. George was alone again.

But, for the moment, a humbled George. He had been in the wrong. Wrong over the absurdest trifle, no doubt, but still—wrong. Unfair. And unfair, he realized, to Olivia no less than to Anne. For he had been blaming Olivia in his thoughts, telling himself that, if the house was badly run, it was the fault of the mistress. 'Really, Olivia if a man can't have matches in his own house—' And there they were, a box for him wherever he might be. How well she looked after him!

He sat down, pulling luxuriously at his pipe, and began to consider his position. Indeed, he told himself to do this in so many words: 'I must consider my position.' And considering it now fairly, reasonably, under the comforting influence of tobacco, and still with that unwonted touch of humility upon him, he found that, in whatever direction his thoughts started out, down whatever side-tracks they wandered, they came back always to the beacon-light of Olivia's presence in the house. She was here. He was angry with her; he was quarrelling with her;

yes, but these were trifles compared with the great fact that she was here to be quarrelled with. She was dictating to him; yes, but here she was to dictate. She was here. In his house ...

In his house, yes; but that was not much comfort if he were elsewhere. And he would have to be elsewhere, unless he surrendered to her. Impossible to force this second marriage on her; impossible, after all that he had said, to remain in the house if she refused it. His whole protest had been that it was the wrongness of it, not, as she had implied, the fear of what the County would say, which forbade them living together unmarried. It was impossible to go back on that, the moment that the circumstances changed. Now the County would never know; nobody would know except Aunt Julia; but right was still right (as he had maintained) and wrong was wrong. If he betrayed his beliefs now, he betrayed himself doubly. At whatever cost, he must cling to them.

The only alternative, then, was to marry her on her own terms. Yes, it must come to that. Already he saw himself surrendering to her. Whatever her conditions, he must accept them. So comforting was the tobacco, so warm the thought that she was here, in his house, and would never leave it now, that he actually chuckled for a moment at her cleverness. She dictating to him! The cheek of her, the cleverness of her! A beauty she had always been, but, gad, she was clever, too. No one to touch her in the county. And his! His now for ever.

But if he was to give way to her on this matter of Dinah's engagement, it was necessary to assure himself first that she was in the right about it. Never should it be said of George that he had sacrificed Dinah's happiness to his own; that he had allowed her to make an impossible marriage simply in order that he might win Olivia's favour. He was a reasonable man, was George. Convince him that Dinah would be happy with young Strange—her happiness, that was all he wanted—and the marriage should take place. Convince him that she would not be happy, and young Strange should be sent about his business. He had feared that morning that young Strange was not suited to Dinah; perhaps he had been wrong? Surely Olivia, who knew young Strange so much better than he—Olivia, who was so intimately in Dinah's confidence—surely her opinion on this matter was worth considering? If Olivia thought that Dinah and young Strange would be happy together, it was his duty, as Dinah's guardian, not to reject this happiness for his ward too hastily. An engagement—there would be no harm, at any rate, in an engagement.

He was now reassured. With a clear conscience he could agree to Olivia's conditions. No, not conditions. It just happened that Dinah would now be 'getting married herself soon,' and that, in some way, this would 'make things easier.' Women were strange creatures. There was no accounting for their whims. However, one had to humour them. It wasn't as if they had the cool reasoning powers, the stern logical faculty, of men.

He got up and went to the window to knock the ashes out of his pipe. How peaceful the lawns looked, how beautiful the wooded hills beyond. All his. His and Olivia's.

II

Our last view of Mr. Pim (such are our privileges) was from Olivia's bedroom window. We saw George bidding him an enthusiastic good-bye; we seemed to see Mr. Pim still maintaining that he had been put to no trouble at all, and that he would on such a beautiful afternoon enjoy the little walk to the Trevors'. 'You mean the Brymers',' we can imagine George correcting him, to which Mr. Pim answered, no doubt, 'Yes, yes, of course, the Brymers'. I am going back to the Brymers'.' Then he was off. We watched him ambling down the drive, until the bend of it hid him from our sight.

Let us be after him. We have the others under our hands when we want them. Olivia is in the morning-room putting the finishing touches to her curtains, and wondering, with half a smile, how long it will be before George comes back to her—five minutes or ten? George is in the library, nervous but determined; telling himself that if it were ten minutes rather than five, he could rehearse something sufficiently casual and off-hand, yet clothed withal in a certain dignity. He tries over a sentence or two; we shall see how it goes directly. Brian and Dinah are wrapt in lovers' talk up and down the rose-garden. As for Lady Marden, to whom we may now wave 'Good-bye,' she is ten fields away or more, and moving splendidly. Let her go; we shall not want her again. Our business is with Mr. Pim.

Somebody has said—with what authority I do not know—that everything which we see or do or hear, even perhaps think, is recorded somewhere in our brain. There the record remains, locked up, the key, it may be, lost, the secret spring hidden, until the day when chance or an effort of will puts it again into our hands. This may be a comforting thought to some, but to the man with a bad memory it brings small consolation. Yet it consoled Mr. Pim. Indeed, it did more than console him; it assured him that he had an excellent memory. He was continually remembering things. Sometimes it was an address which he had forgotten forty years ago, sometimes a name which he had heard yesterday; and each accidental opening of a secret drawer emphasized for him the value of the treasures still hidden, and gave a new excitement to the next opening.

We catch him up as he stands at the gate, and we see at once that something has happened. He has stood there, one hand on the latch, old eyes to the green roof above him with its pattern of sunlight coming through, ever since we had him first in sight; stood there, thinking, thinking. Suddenly he nods to himself; a happy smile illumines his face. He has remembered. The eyes come down, the hand presses down the latch, the gate begins to swing open before him. He follows it ...

But he does not pass through. Step by step he retreats, the gate pressing after him. Now it is shut again, and he is still on the Marden House side of it. Happiness has gone from his face; other emotions have taken charge of it: Horror, Shame, Doubt. A second time he presses down the latch; Doubt has made way for Relief. The gate begins to open again; then Relief fades out. Doubt returns. Once more the gate urges him back. Doubt has gone. Resolution triumphs in every line of him. The latch clicks ... and Mr. Pim, turning bravely round, walks back to Marden House.

III

'May I come in, Mrs. Marden?'

Olivia dropped her curtains, and looked round in astonishment at the windows. Mr. Pim again! He stood on the terrace, nervously waiting permission to enter, and his eyes strayed from her to the door, and then back to her again, and then over his shoulder as if wondering whether a return to the gate would not be the best course after all.

'Come in, Mr. Pim,' said Olivia, surprise in her voice.

He still hesitated.

'Mr. Marden is not here?'

She made a movement as if to get up, and he retreated a step.

'Do you want to see him?' she asked. 'I will—'

'No, no, no' he interrupted her hastily. 'Not for the world.'

She took up her curtains again, and invited him with a smile to come in. He stepped in carefully. As he came opposite the door he stopped, and seemed to be measuring the distance between it and the window.

'There is no immediate danger of his returning?' he asked.

'No, I don't think so. Why, what is it?'

'I took the liberty of returning by the window in the hope of coming upon you alone, Mrs. Marden.'

'Yes. Do sit down, won't you?'

He drew up a chair, near to her, yet not too far from the window, and sat down on the edge of it.

'I—er—the fact is—' He looked down at his hat, with which his fingers played nervously, and then up at her over the top of his spectacles, imploring her aid. She gave him a smile, sympathetic, friendly, comforting.

'Mr. Marden will be very angry with me,' he said, shaking his head at her, almost reproachfully, as if she were forgiving him too soon. 'Quite rightly. Oh, quite rightly. I blame myself entirely. I do not know how I can have been so stupid.'

'But what is it, Mr. Pim?' Then with a little laugh, for the danger was past, and seemed so very far away now, she asked, 'Has my husband come to life again?'

'Mrs. Marden, I throw myself on your mercy entirely. The fact is'—he bent over his hat until it was close to his eyes, brushed off a speck of dust, and then, straightening himself suddenly, said—'his name was Polwittle.'

'Whose?' said Olivia, trying bravely not to laugh. 'My husband's?'

He nodded eagerly.

'Yes, yes. The name came back to me suddenly just as I reached the gate. Polwittle. Poor fellow!'

'Mr. Pim,' said Olivia, in her most soothing voice, yet wondering what it was all about, 'my husband's name was Telworthy.'

He shook his head vigorously.

'No, no, Polwittle.'

'But really,' protested Olivia, laughing, 'I ought to know.'

'Polwittle,' said Mr. Pim, almost fretfully this time. They were trying to muddle him. They had made the whole story very difficult for him, and it was *his* story. 'Polwittle!

It came back to me suddenly just as I reached the gate. For the moment I—er—I had thoughts of conveying the news by letter. I was naturally disinclined to return in person, and—er—yes, Polwittle.' Modestly pleased with his astonishing memory, he added, 'If you remember, I always said it was a peculiar name.'

For once Olivia was a little slow. 'But who is Polwittle?' she asked.

'The man I have been telling you about, of course. The man whom I met on the boat, who came to such a sad end at Marseilles.'

Olivia stared at him, unable to say anything.

'Henry Polwittle,' he murmured happily. 'Henry—' He stopped, and frowned at the ceiling. 'Or was it Ernest?' he wondered. Then his face cleared, and he said with decision, 'No, Henry, I think. Poor fellow!'

'But you said his name was Telworthy,' she burst out. 'How could you?'

'Yes, yes, I blame myself entirely.'

'But how could you *think* of a name like Telworthy, if it wasn't Telworthy?'

He shook his finger at her eagerly.

'Ah, that is the really interesting thing about the whole affair,' he assured her, now quite happy again, and he nodded his old head in confirmation of it.

'Mr. Pim,' she said gravely, a smile hovering, 'all your visits to-day have been—interesting.' How absurd, and how absurd, and then again how *absurd* it was!

The irony passed him by. He went on eagerly. 'Yes, but you see, on my first appearance here this morning I was received by Miss Diana.'

'Dinah.' She would have to laugh soon.

'Miss Dinah, yes. She was in rather a communicative mood, and she happened to mention, by way of passing the time, that before your marriage to Mr. Marden you had been a Mrs.—er—'

'Telworthy.'

'Telworthy, yes. She mentioned also Australia. By some process of the brain, which strikes me as decidedly curious, when I was trying to recollect the name of the poor fellow on the boat, whom, you remember, I had also met in Australia, the fact that this other name was now stored in my memory in conjunction with that same country—this fact, I say—this fact—'

It was obvious that there was no hope of a sentence begun like this ever coming to a respectable end. But its meaning had emerged; and in answer to his appealing look, Olivia put it out of its misery.

'Yes, yes,' she said. 'I understand.'

So that was it! She was still Mrs. Marden; she had always been Mrs. Marden. Dinah's chatter, an old man's elusive memory—from such little causes had sprung the Great Event. But Mr. Pim had paid his fourth visit, and now everything was just as it was before he began to come.

Well, no. Everything was not just as it was. One could not blot out the day as if it had never happened. The position was the same, but the protagonists were different. Olivia was not the Olivia of the morning, nor George the George. What would be the effect of that? Husband and wife were at odds this morning about Dinah's engagement and other small matters. Would the new Olivia and the new George be in any closer agreement?

Olivia imagined him receiving the news. 'It's all right, I *am* your wife after all. The whole thing was a mistake.' His wife after all! What could he feel but resentment for the fright she had given him, and an increased hardening towards her wishes for her failure to force them upon him? What could she show but an abiding wound caused by his betrayal of her? Neither of them would forget now, nor forgive. The quarrel (hateful word, but there was no other) would remain unfinished. How much better if she had been left to smooth it, and pat it, and round it off in her own way.

'I blame myself, I blame myself entirely,' Mr. Pim was murmuring.

She blamed him, too; not for his mistake, but for this attempt to wipe out his mistake. If only he had waited a day or two longer! But this was so unfair that she had to smile at herself, and say, with all her charm, 'Oh, you mustn't do that, Mr. Pim. It was really Dinah's fault for inflicting all our family history on you.'

'Oh, but a delightful young woman! I assure you I was very much interested in all that she told me.' He got slowly to his feet. 'Well, Mrs. Marden, I can only hope that you will forgive me for the needless distress I have caused you to-day.'

'Oh, you mustn't worry about that, please,' she begged him, smiling her forgiveness.

He looked anxiously at the door.

'And you will tell your husband? You will—er—break the news to him?'

She gave a little start; wrinkled her brow in a sudden thought; stared at him, lips parted. Then a smile began to peep out of her eyes, adorably mischievous; peeped out and whisked back again on the instant.

'I will break the news to him,' she said demurely.

'You understand how it is that I thought it better to come to you in the first place?'

Again the smile gleamed and was gone.

'I am very glad you did,' she said.

He held out his hand, satisfied now that he had done his duty.

'Then I will say good-bye, Mrs. Marden.'

She was as eager now as he that he should be gone before George came back. But she must be certain that it was really 'Good-bye' this time.

'Just a moment, Mr. Pim,' she said. 'Let us have it quite clear this time.' She looked him straight in the face. 'You never knew my husband, Jacob Telworthy. You never met him in Australia. You never saw him on the boat. Nothing whatever happened to him at Marseilles. Is that right?'

Mr. Pim blinked rapidly at each statement, and hurried on after the next. He arrived breathless at the finishing point, having just managed to keep up with her.

'Yes, yes, that is so.' They were hurrying him, they were hurrying him again.

She went on inexorably: 'So that, since he was presumed to have died in Australia six years ago, he is presumably still dead?'

'Yes, yes, undoubtedly.'

Counsel sat down suddenly, cross-examination finished, and hostess, all smiles and friendliness, stepped forward.

'Then, good-bye, Mr. Pim,' she said. 'And thank you so much for—for all your trouble.'

He was apologizing again, assuring her that it was no trouble at all, but a fresh young voice from the terrace put all that out of his head, and renewed his anxiety to be gone.

'Hallo, here's Mr. Pim!' cried Dinah.

She came in, the faithful Brian attending. 'He's just met my second husband,' she whispered over her shoulder. 'Be decent about it, Brian.'

'Yes, yes,' said Mr. Pim, nervously, trying to get past her before George should come back. 'I—er—'

'Oh, but Mr. Pim, you mustn't run away without even saying how do you do. Such old friends as we are. Why it's ages since we last met. Are you staying to tea?'

'No, no, I'm afraid that—er—' He looked round appealingly to Olivia. A delightful young woman, Miss Diana, but—

'Mr. Pim has to hurry away, dear,' said Olivia, no less anxious. 'You mustn't keep him.'

'Well, but you will come back again?'

'I fear that I am only a passer-by, Miss Diana.'

'Dinah.'

'Er—Dinah.'

'You can walk with him to the gate, darling.'

'Right-o,' said Dinah. Mr. Pim glanced his thanks to his hostess and went eagerly to the window.

'Are you coming, Brian?'

'I'll catch you up.'

'Come along then, Mr. Pim.' She took his arm. 'Now I want to hear all about your *first* wife. You really haven't told me anything yet.'

'But I'm not married,' he said, chuckling at her mistake.

'Oh nonsense,' protested the smiling Dinah.

Once more Mr. Pim negotiated the steps of the terrace. But quite happily now. Oh, a most delightful young woman.

IV

If one were permitted to generalize about woman—always a dangerous thing to do, and very annoying to woman—one would say that her emotions were less diffused than man's. She feels what she feels with a more concentrated energy. Brian loved Dinah as deeply as she loved him, but he had room in his heart for emotions which were crowded out of hers by the new happiness which had invaded it. She loved him; he loved her; that was all that there was in her world. He loved her; she loved him; in his world there was everything which had been there before, but, in the new light by which he now saw it, a thousand times more beautiful, a thousand times more pitiful. The more he loved, the more love he had to give; the more she loved, the less love she had to spare. For Dinah, Brian was now the only man; for Brian every woman now showed something of Dinah.

So, while the girl went off happily with Mr. Pim, her lover waited behind with the beautiful, the pitiful, Olivia. A week ago he would have been sorry, sympathetic, kind. 'How awful!' he would have said, not really awed, or no more than he habitually was by a bad picture or a fluke at billiards. But to-day Olivia's tragedy was Dinah's tragedy, his tragedy, Love's universal tragedy. Confronted with it, what lover could be happy?

Awkwardly he went up to her and touched her hand.

'I just wanted to say,' he stammered, 'if—if you don't think it cheek—that—that'—he could think of no better expression of his feelings than the phrase he had used before—'that I'm on your side, if I may be.'

She looked at him affectionately, tears almost in her eyes. 'Oh, Brian,' she said.

'Of course, I don't suppose I can do anything,' he went on, 'but if I *could* help you, I should be awfully proud of being allowed to.'

'You dear. That's sweet of you.' Now a tear did come. She put a handkerchief to it, and said brightly: 'But it's quite all right now, you know.'

To Brian this naturally meant that George had at last decided to do 'the one and only thing.' His face lit up.

'Oh, I say, how splendid!' he said. 'I'm awfully glad.'

'Yes, that's why Mr. Pim came back. He found that he had made a mistake about the name.'

Brian gaped at her.

'A mistake about the name?' he stuttered, incredulous.

'Yes. George is the only husband I have.'

'You mean that the whole thing—you mean that Pim never—well,' he ended up with conviction, 'of all the silly asses!' He stared through the windows after that disappearing gentleman. 'You ass!' he murmured, shaking his head at him. Then, coming back to Olivia, he said eagerly, 'I say, I'm *awfully* glad.'

'Thank you, Brian, dear.'

So Brian knew now. He was bound to know anyhow, if Mr. Pim mentioned it to Dinah, as easily he might. And if Brian and Dinah knew, how could George be kept from knowing?

For George was not to know. Not yet. Olivia was determined to wind up the affair in her own way, just as if Mr. Pim had never come back. George should marry her on her own conditions. He had been prepared to sacrifice her to his prejudices; now he must be prepared to sacrifice his prejudices to her. Only so they could live together as equals, neither of them ashamed, neither of them resentful. The affair must finish in the grand manner, white flag flying, trumpets blowing, curtains hanging. 'A good lunch somewhere' would mark its end. With the good lunch everything would be forgiven and forgotten.

But then, how could George be kept from knowing that the affair was already over? Olivia smiled at the easiness of it. Let the children talk as much as they liked. George would never know, until she told him. She had her plan for that. Oh, but it was easy!

'Brian,' she said suddenly, 'do you know anything about the Law?'

That distinguished young painter admitted, with a certain pride, that he knew nothing about the Law. He detested the Law. But why was Olivia worrying about it?

'Oh, I was just wondering. Thinking about all the shocks we have been through to-day. Second marriages, you know, and all that sort of thing.'

Brian nodded. 'It's a rotten business,' he agreed.

'I suppose,' said Olivia, busy with her curtains, 'that there's nothing wrong—legally wrong, I mean—in getting married to the *same* person twice?'

'A hundred times if you like, I should think,' he answered carelessly.

'The Law is so funny about things.'

'After all, in France they always go through it twice, don't they? Once before the Mayor or somebody, and once in Church.'

'Of course they do! How silly of me!' She smiled to herself as she went on. 'I think they ought to do it in England more. I think it's rather a nice idea.' Her smile deepened as she saw herself and George inaugurating this nice idea. George not quite realizing what a nice idea it was.

Brian was not much interested in these philosophical speculations about the value of double marriages. The important matter was not how many times you married, but whom you married.

'Well, once will be enough for Dinah and me,' he said, 'if you can work it.'

Olivia, still pondering her plans with that smile upon her face, said nothing.

'Of course,' he added hurriedly, 'if you're keen on our doing it three or four times, at three or four different places, we shall be there.' He came closer to her and said, 'I say, Olivia, is there any chance? Or have I torn it entirely by what I said—oh, well, you don't want to talk about that now.'

'There is every chance, dear,' she said. It was all part of the smile.

'I say, is there really?' He bent down impetuously and kissed her cheek. 'By Jove! you really are a wonder. Have you squared him? No, I don't mean that. Sorry. I mean—'

She patted his arm gently.

'Go and catch Dinah up. We will talk about it later on. But everything is going to be all right,' She hesitated a moment. 'And, Brian?'

'Yes?'

It was difficult to say what she wanted to say. Perhaps, anyhow, she oughtn't to say it.

'Yes?' said Brian again.

With an adorable little laugh, half shy, half amused, she said:

'I rather like George, you know.'

'Oh, Olivia! I'm a beast. Oh, you dear! Bless you.' He stammered at her awkwardly, and then, coming round to the front of the sofa, bent and kissed her hand. After which display of emotion the only thing to do was to get out of the room as quickly as possible, with the explanation that he would catch them up.

As he went, the man whom Olivia rather liked came in.

Chapter Fourteen
A Good Little Boy

There were six more rings to go on, and then the curtains were finished. Olivia picked up the last but five, held it in position and began to sew. Somewhere behind her was the man she rather liked. He was at a disadvantage, because he had no curtains to sew. The strain of saying nothing would tell upon him first. He would have to begin ...

He walked across the room, humming carelessly to himself. Arrived at the fire-place, he bent down and knocked out his pipe against his heel carelessly. From this position he stole a glance at Olivia under his arm to see if she were looking at him. Her eyes were on her needle. There! Another ring finished. She turned for the last but four, and George's eyes went hastily back to his heel. There was a *crescendo* effect in his humming, given with the abandon of the true artist. 'Jolly afternoon, this,' he seemed to be saying. 'I wonder what Olivia's doing? Down in the garden picking roses, no doubt. Might stroll down there myself.'

Confound it, why didn't she say something? He tried again to catch her eye, and then, in a sudden panic, tried to avoid it. Suppose she did begin? Suppose she said 'Well, George?' What could he say? Nothing but 'Well, Olivia?'—and then, where were you? Nowhere. It would be better if he began himself. Casually. Er—by the way—

He was at the windows now, drawn there by an instinctive need for air. As he had said, he could see as well as anybody in the county. Between bushes he had a glimpse of Brian hurrying gaily after his beloved one, and even at that distance the glow of happiness on his face, the easy carriage, the charming youth of him was visible to George. Almost involuntarily he muttered, 'H'm! Good-looking fellow, young Strange,' and with the words realized that he had made a beginning.

Olivia, you may be sure, was ready for it.

'Brian, yes, isn't he?' she said carelessly. 'And such a nice boy.' The nice boy had disappeared now round the corner of the drive, but George continued to gaze after him.

'Got fifty pounds for a picture the other day, didn't you tell me?' he said, apparently to somebody on the terrace.

'Yes,' said Olivia, to her curtains. 'Of course, he has only just begun,' she told the last ring but three.

'Critics think well of him, what?'

'They all say he has genius,' Olivia informed the scissors. 'Oh, I don't think there's any doubt of it.'

George nodded to his informant on the terrace.

'Of course,' he said, with the air of one making a great concession, 'I don't profess to know anything about painting.'

Olivia reminded the curtains that he had never had the time to take it up.

'I know what I like, of course,' said George, thereby singling himself out from the rest of us. The trouble with the rest of us is that we know what other people tell us we ought to like, and pretend to like it. 'I know what I like, and I can't say I see much in this new-fangled stuff. If a man can paint, why can't he paint like'—he frowned for a moment over the fellow's name—'like Rubens? Or'—he was in a magnanimous mood—'like Reynolds?'

Why indeed? However, Olivia was able to suggest a possible reason.

'I suppose we all have our own styles,' she said.

He agreed eagerly. Yes, no doubt, that would be it.

'Brian will find his style directly,' she went on. 'He's only just beginning.'

'But the critics think a lot of him, what?'

'Oh, yes!'

'Ah!'

It was very reassuring that the critics thought a lot of him, because the critics, it was well known, were mostly middle-aged men. Men of George's age; men whose opinions, therefore, were of value. Sound men. The critic of *The Times* for instance, or of the *Morning Post*, would certainly be a man, a middle-aged man, of position and learning; possibly of family. If such a man thought well of young Strange, there was hope for the fellow. And a good-looking fellow, too. Not one of these bearded anarchists, like so many of them.

He came away from the windows well pleased with himself. Things were going well; not quite as he had imagined them (they never go like that), but without embarrassment for either. He was convinced now that he could trust Dinah safely to this promising young artist. Naturally, he wanted to be sure of this before giving his consent to the engagement. If Olivia were worrying about Dinah, she need worry no more. He began to hum again; the happy, careless hum of a man who had got something off his mind and was now at ease again; the hum of a man whose wife might now be at ease again also.

But there was just one other little matter to be put right, one other little matter over which, it might be, Olivia was worrying. He leant against a chair, filling his pipe, and when all was ready for the match, he said, as he drew out the box:

'Nearly finished 'em?'

'Very nearly,' she assured him. Then looking round, 'Are my scissors there?'

'Scissors?' He was all eagerness to find them for her.

'Ah, here they are.' She had them all the time, but she wanted him to feel that he was helping her. He seemed to her like a little boy, who has been bad, but is now trying to be very good, so that nothing shall be said about his badness. Little boy! She longed to kiss him and tell him that it was all right now. Very soon it would be all right now, and then she would kiss him. Funny little boy!

His pipe was now lighted. He walked across to the fire-place which was waiting for the match-end, and, as he went, he asked the great question.

'Where are you going to put 'em?'

It was the question, so it seemed to Olivia at that moment, up to which all Mr. Pim's visits—three, or was it four?—had slowly but inevitably been leading Why, she asked herself whimsically, had he come at all, if not to hang her curtains for her? 'What shall we do about Olivia's curtains?' one of the Household Gods had asked on Olympus. 'That fellow George won't let her hang them in the morning-room.' And they had looked down, and seen a little old gentleman getting into a train at Paddington. 'Why, that's just the man you want,' said a second god. 'Meeting the girl first, of course?' said the other. 'Meeting the girl first, of course,' he agreed. And so now her curtains were going up. What a funny old world it was!

But she appreciated the way in which George had put it. Any previous argument about the curtains was wiped out. There had been no mention of them before; indeed, it was doubtful if he had even seen them. Seeing them now for the first time, he naturally asked her where she was going to put them.

'I don't quite know,' she said, looking at them thoughtfully, head on one side. Evidently she, too, was now giving them her attention for the first time. 'I had thought of this room, but'—she frowned at them—'I'm not quite sure.' She was still, it seemed, open to suggestion.

George suggested casually that they would brighten the room up a bit.

'Yes,' said Olivia doubtfully.

He walked over to the windows and examined the curtains now hanging there. He had never really looked at them before. There they had always been, ever since he could remember; as a boy he had pulled at them, tripped over them, hidden behind them. If you had asked him suddenly what colour they were, I doubt whether he could have told you. But they were part of the room, and the room was part of the house, and the house was part of his inheritance, entrusted to him by his father and his grandfather and his great-grandfather, and, as Dinah had said, all the rest of them. No, not his room now; that was where he had been wrong; his and Olivia's.

'Well, yes,' he admitted, surprise in his voice, 'they *are* a bit faded.'

Olivia held her own curtains up and had a good look at them. The curtains were a moral triumph without doubt, but she was not certain now that they were an artistic one. She was in that state of indecision to which every artist comes sooner or later. We look at our new masterpiece, and we say, as she said now to George, 'Sometimes I think I love it, and sometimes—I'm not quite sure.'

'The best way,' he suggested, 'is to hang them up and see how you like them then. Always take them down again.'

She looked at him with admiration.

'That's rather a good idea, George.'

'Best way,' said George, pleased to be so helpful. He was a little surprised that Olivia had not thought of it herself. It was the obvious thing.

'Yes,' she said, 'I think we might do that. The only thing is—'

'What?' said George, seeing her hesitate.

'Well, the carpet and the chairs and the cushions and things.'

'What about 'em?' For the moment he was a little slow.

'Well, if you had new curtains—' She waited for him. He was there at once.

'You mean we'd want a new carpet,' he said triumphantly.

'Yes. Well, new chair-covers, anyhow.'

'Well, why not?'

How good, how very good the bad little boy was being!

'Oh, but—'

'We're not so hard up as all that, you know,' he said, a little awkwardly. This was uncomfortable talk, dangerously reminiscent of certain conversations which, they were agreed now, had never taken place.

'No, I suppose not,' said Olivia, with a smile for herself only.

'That's all right,' he said cheerfully.

But still, unaccountably, she hesitated.

'I suppose it would mean that I should have to go up to London for them. That's rather a nuisance.'

'Oh, I don't know,' he said, more casual now than ever. Hands in pockets, eyes on the floor, he moved across the room, falling slowly from one foot to the other. 'We might go up together one day.'

'Well, of course, if we *were* up for anything else'—she stole a glance at him—'we could just look about us, and see if we could find what we want.'

'That's what I meant. If we *were* up—for anything else.'

'Exactly,' said Olivia.

He gave a sigh of relief. He had done his part; tactfully, delicately. Everything was now comfortable; misunderstandings had been removed. It only remained to settle about this 'something else' which might demand their presence in London. To propose to her again, in fact. He cleared his throat warningly.

But Olivia had not finished playing her part. For just a little longer George must be kept in ignorance of the truth—the truth which by now was known to that chatter-box Dinah. There was only one way of doing this. Was it quite—well, quite honourable? All was fair in love and war, and this was a mixture of both. A wise woman keeps her husband in ignorance of many things; for his own good, of course. This was for George's own good, but was it quite—? Anyhow, it was rather fun; a joke; perhaps that saved it.

'Oh, by the way, George,' she said, before he could begin, 'I told Brian—and that means telling Dinah, of course—that Mr. Pim had made a mistake about the name.'

He stared at her. He could only repeat the words after her, not realizing yet what they meant.

'Yes,' she nodded. 'I told Brian that the whole thing was a mistake.'

Slowly he understood her, or thought that he understood. 'Olivia!' he cried eagerly.

How misleading the truth is! She had uttered no more, no less, than the truth—that she had told Brian that Mr. Pim had made a mistake. But accepting this as the truth, George, as Olivia had foreseen, put his own construction upon it. He assumed that she had misled Brian in order to make things easy for them.

'Olivia! Then you mean that Brian and Dinah think that we have been married all the time?'

'Yes,' she smiled. 'They both think so now.'

He came very close to her. There could be only one reason for Olivia's brilliant diplomacy.

'Does that mean,' he asked shyly, 'that you *are* thinking of marrying me?'

'At your old registry office?'

'Yes!'

'To-morrow?'

'Yes!'

How eager, how happy he was, this good little boy who had been so bad.

'Do you want me to *very* much?'

'My darling,' he cried, 'you know that I do.'

She had a moment of apprehension. In spite of Brian's contempt of the Law, in spite of France's nice ideas about marriage ceremonies, she was still a little anxious as to whether the great joke could be carried off.

'We should have to do it very quietly,' she warned him.

'Of course, darling,' he agreed eagerly. 'Nobody need know at all. We don't want anybody to know. And now that you have put Brian and Dinah off the scent by telling them that Mr. Pim made a mistake—' He stopped, and looked at her with admiration. What diplomacy! What a brain! 'That was very clever of you, Olivia,' he said gravely. 'I should never have thought of that.'

'No, darling.' Then anxiously, 'You don't think it was wrong, George?'

George, the man with the conscience, the authority on what the Law, Heaven, and the Best People really thought, Justice of the Peace in the County of Buckinghamshire, delivered his verdict.

'An innocent deception, my dear. Perfectly harmless.'

Olivia breathed again.

'Yes,' she said, 'that was what I thought about—about what I was doing.'

Now let Dinah chatter as she would. George, on this matter, was truth-proof. In an hour he would be in the train on his way to London; in twenty-four hours, if it could be arranged by then, they would be married again, 'very quietly.' And then? Well, then perhaps she would tell him the truth. What fun!

'Then you will come to-morrow?' he asked, very close to her now.

She nodded.

'And if we happen to see a carpet, or anything that you want—'

'Oh, how lovely!' she cried.

She was like a child herself now, clapping her hands at the treats in store for her. He felt the joy of making this child happy.

'And a wedding-lunch at the Carlton?' he beamed.

Again her excited nod.

'And a bit of a honeymoon in Paris?'

This was almost too much. 'Oh, George!' she cried.

He put out his arms to her.

'Give us a kiss, old girl,' he asked, humbly, entreatingly, hungrily; asking, with the words, forgiveness for the past, promising happiness for the future. A kiss as a sign that they were back to the old comfortable friendly times again, when 'Olivia' was a warm glow at the heart, not a dull ache. Olivia, be friends!

And now her arms were round him, comforting him, taking him back. 'My dear!' she murmured.

'Don't ever leave me, old girl,' he prayed.

'Don't ever send me away, old boy,' she said.

'I won't!' he cried fervently. And then, remembering with shame how nearly he had done it, he said awkwardly, eyes hidden from her, 'I—I don't think I would have, you know.'

Little boy!

Chapter Fifteen

The Curtains Go Up

I

Brian caught them up at the gate. They stood there for a little, the three of them, saying good-bye.

'You must come and see us next time you're down, Mr. Pim,' said Dinah firmly. 'Promise!'

'It is very kind of you, Miss Marden, but I may not be in these parts again.'

'Oh, nonsense! I'll tell Mr. Brymer that he's got to ask you again. He's a great friend of mine.'

'But I have my work in London, you must remember.'

'Brian, Mr. Pim lives with his sister in London, and her name's Prudence. Prudence Pim—isn't it lovely? I'm sure she's a perfect darling. She's coming to tea with me when we're married.'

'I hope Mr. Pim will come, too,' said Brian, smiling pleasantly at him.

'Thank you, thank you.'

'We shall live in Chelsea,' explained Dinah. 'Brian, how far is that from Bloomsbury?'

'Not too far for Mr. Pim, I hope.'

'I have been a great traveller, Miss Marden. As I was telling Mrs. Marden, I have only recently arrived from Australia.'

He chuckled to himself. 'I have no doubt I could manage the journey to Chelsea. And Prudence, too.' He chuckled again to find that he had the young people laughing with him.

'Very well, then, that's settled,' said Dinah. 'Tell Miss Pim that that is the very first invitation to my new house which I have issued. Which I have issued,' she repeated to Brian. 'Doesn't it sound grand? Like royalty.'

She laughed again out of simple happiness, the laugh which thrilled Brian, and held out her hand to Mr. Pim.

'Good-bye, Mr. Pim.'

'Good-bye, sir,' added Brian.

He took off his hat and bowed courteously, first over Dinah's hand, then over Brian's.

'Good-bye, good-bye,' he said. 'God bless you both.' And so through the gate and, for the last time surely, out of Marden House.

Dinah's farewell wave lacked finish, she was so eager to talk to Brian alone.

'I say,' she began excitedly, 'did you know that the whole thing—I mean Telworthy—'

He nodded.

'Olivia's just told me. Isn't it absurd?'

'I knew things like that didn't really happen. Except in books, of course.'

'But I can tell you something which really is going to happen,' said Brian, looking at her fondly.

'Us? You and me? Why, of course it is.'

'I mean George and you and me.'

'He's relented?'

'Yes.'

'Have you seen him?'

'No, but Olivia told me. Well, practically told me.'

He beamed at her, as if he had done it all himself, and waited for her exclamation of delight. But Dinah was not so sure that she was delighted. The part of the unhappy maiden immured by the wicked uncle had its attractions. Not for her now the clandestine meeting; not for her the notes left under doormats, the tryst by the withered thorn when all the household was asleep. All the romance of the forbidden engagement was torn from her. Alas, alas!

'What is it, darling?' asked her lover, seeing that something was wrong.

She shook her head. Absurd tears were gathering unbidden.

'Sweetheart!' His arms went round her.

'Oh, Brian!' She clung to him. 'I don't know what's the matter. Let me be silly sometimes. It's because I love you so. There's such a lot about love; it makes you want so much … and—not want it … and not know what you want.'

'Sweetheart,' he said again. What else could he say?

'I want you like this—with me, and I want you far away from me, so that I can think about you. It's all a new country, and there are so many ways to go—all beautiful. I think that's why I am crying, because I don't want to miss any of them. Let me be silly sometimes.'

'But you aren't being,' he protested. 'You're being sweet. You're making me love you more every moment.' He held her tightly to him.

In a small stifled voice she said, 'I think you will have to let me go now, because I want to get at my pocket handkerchief.'

With a laugh he released her. She dabbed at her eyes, smiling at him round the handkerchief. He wanted to protest again that she wasn't being silly, that he quite understood, that he loved her all the more for feeling as she did. But apparently she had forgotten all that.

'The worst of having a nose much too small like mine' she said, 'is that—'

'It isn't too small. It's just the right size.'

'The worst of having a nose just the right size like mine is that when it gets red at the end, then it's practically red all over.'

'It isn't red.'

'Isn't it really? I'm generally an awful sight when I cry.'

He kissed it lightly. 'Now it isn't,' he said.

'Hooray!' She held out a friendly little hand to him. 'Come along, and let's forgive George. He's going to be your uncle. What luck the Mardens have!'

Hand in hand they went up the drive, chattering; Dinah, her own irresponsible self again. But an unwonted humility had descended upon Brian. Somehow he felt that he had let Dinah down; that he had just not said the right thing. 'Lord' he reflected solemnly, 'it's an exciting life.'

II

They were just in time to see Olivia in George's arms.

'Oo, I say!' Dinah burst out.

George freed himself hurriedly, and turned to them as if he had never kissed anybody in his life, but Dinah was not going to let the moment go.

'Give me one, too, George,' she demanded, rushing up to him. 'Brian won't mind.'

This was too much for that young man. 'Really, Dinah, you are the limit,' he said uncomfortably.

But George, happy George, good little boy again, was in his best form now. He held out his hand to his niece, twinkles in his eyes, in the lines of his handsome face.

'Do you mind, Mr. Strange?' he asked politely.

Dinah gave them her own incomparable laugh. Olivia smiled happily on her handsome husband. Only Brian was not quite at his ease. He stammered out something which might or might not have been his permission.

'We'll risk it, Dinah,' said her uncle, and pulled her towards him.

'There!' she said, emerging triumphantly. 'Did you notice that one? That wasn't just an ordinary affectionate uncle kiss. It was a special bless-you-my-children one.' She appealed confidently to George. 'Wasn't it?'

'You do talk nonsense, darling,' said happy Olivia.

'Absolute nonsense,' agreed the happy George.

'It's because everything's so lovely now,' she explained to her aunt. 'I mean now that Mr. Pim has relented about your first husband.'

George and Olivia exchanged a glance. He smiled; how easily Dinah had been taken in. She smiled; how easily George had been taken in. But George thought that it was the same smile as his.

'Yes, yes, stupid fellow, Pim—what?' he said, carrying the joke on.

'Absolute idiot,' agreed Brian.

George's hearty laugh rang out. The joke was too good to be bottled up inside him. But Olivia's joke, so much the better one, still kept within the corners of her mouth and her half-lowered eyes.

'And now that George,' Dinah went on calmly, 'has relented about *my* first husband—'

'Wait a bit,' he protested good-humouredly. 'You get on much too fast, young woman.' He looked across at Brian. 'So you want to marry my Dinah, eh?'

'Well I do rather, sir.'

Dinah elaborated this a little.

'Not at once, of course, George. We want to be engaged for a long time first, and write letters to each other, and tell each other how much we love each other, and sit next to each other when we go out to dinner.' She turned to Brian, and explained hastily: 'You can't sit next to each other when you're married, you know.'

There were so many beautiful ways to go in the new country. She wanted to explore them all, lingeringly, lovingly.

'I see,' said George. He smiled to Olivia. 'Well, that sounds fairly harmless, I think?'

'I think so.'

How easy everything was being made for him, she felt. He beamed upon them in the part of loving husband, indulgent uncle; and behold! it was the only part he had ever played. Automatically they fitted themselves to it; loved wife, indulged niece, propitiatory suitor. How easy everything was always made for men!

'Well, you'd better come and have a talk with me—er—Brian.'

Kind George! Generous George! 'Thank you very much, sir,' said the grateful Brian eagerly.

'Well, come along then. I've got to go up to London after tea'—he looked at his watch—'so we'd better have our little talk now.'

Brian began nervously to estimate his assets, whereof the chief seemed to be young Marshall. If Marshall had bought a picture for fifty pounds, there was no reason why he shouldn't buy another.

'I say, are you going to London?' asked Dinah.

'A little business.' He caught Olivia's eye and laughed happily. 'Never you mind, young woman.'

'All right. Only don't forget my engagement present.'

The indulgent uncle laughed again. The cheek of her!

'Well, well, we'll see. Now then—er—Brian, shall we walk down and look at the pigs?'

'Right-o.'

'Brian and George always discuss me in front of the pigs,' said Dinah to her aunt. 'So tactless of them.'

But there was another reason now why the pigs must be denied this further intimacy with Dinah's affairs.

'Don't go far away, dear,' said Olivia. 'I may want you in a moment.'

George hastened to assent. His one idea was to please everybody. 'We'll be on the terrace,' he said, and led the way out of the windows. Brian followed nervously.

How surprised Father would be if Suitor spoke to him in this fashion. 'I want to marry your daughter. The reasons why I think you can trust her safely to me are as follows: I have a sense of humour, and by the Grace of God it is the same sense of humour as hers. I shall not bore her by repeating what seem to her to be pointless stories which I have heard at the club, nor, on the other hand, will she irritate me by listening with an artificial smile to what seem to me to be delightfully humorous stories. The same people, the same accidents to ourselves or to others, will amuse us. We have already, Heaven be thanked, something of the same feeling as to what is beautiful and what is not beautiful. It is probable that with companionship our tastes will become more nearly identical, I learning from her, and she from me. In any case there is much common ground upon which we can meet. I have, I think, some imagination. I can understand that in any difference between husband and wife there is a woman's point of view as well as a man's; a point of view no less legitimate. I shall try to remember that marriage is a partnership, in which the man is not inevitably the senior partner. If we have children, my memory is not so untrustworthy that I shall forget who suffered to bring them into the world, my sense of humour (to refer to it again) is not so lacking that I shall adopt the airs of the sole proprietor, the only director of their destinies. As regards money matters, if she is dependent on my income for her comforts, I shall remember that it is by my own wish that she is so dependent, and I shall recognize that she has as much right to those comforts as I have. Finally, if I must refer particularly (as seems in these cases to be customary) to that one of the virtues which, for some reason, is singled out as Virtue, I bring to my wife no less than I receive from her; I expect from her no more than I can keep for her. In this matter I recognize no shadow of a difference between the two sexes. Sir, I have the honour to say again that I want to marry your daughter.'

How indignant Father would be if Suitor spoke to him in this fashion. How quickly he would dismiss the ridiculous fellow and send for the next suitor. The next suitor says: 'I want to marry your daughter. I have ten thousand pounds a year in gilt-edged securities, together with other investments which bring in some additional four thousand. When Great-Aunt Agatha dies—she is ninety-three, poor soul, and one cannot wish her sufferings to be prolonged—I come into another three thousand a year. The Jaggers are a very old family, and Sir Eustace Jagger, who may be relied upon to come to the wedding, is my second cousin. Naturally (speaking as one man of the world to another) I have had my little affairs, but they may be regarded now as entirely closed; satisfactorily, I think I may say, to both sides. Sir, I want to marry your daughter.'

How gladly Father shakes him by the hand! Take her, my boy, she is yours!

Wherefore Brian followed George nervously to the terrace, wondering which of his aunts was going to be most useful to him this afternoon.

Olivia was now at the last ring of all. Dinah watched her thoughtfully for the first few stitches, and then said: 'Are you going to London, too?'

'To-morrow morning.'

'What for?'

'Shopping, and—one or two little things.'

'I suppose Brian will go up by your train?'

Olivia nodded.

'Leaving Dinah all alone in the country. Will she mind?'

'No. I want to be alone. Just for a little.' Then suddenly, to the great jeopardy of the last ring of all, her arms went round Olivia, and she was holding her tightly.

'Dinah, darling.'

'That means everything that I can't say,' whispered Dinah. 'Have long talks with me when you come back, will you?'

Olivia promised.

'I didn't really mean that about an engagement present, you know.'

'Dearest one,' said Olivia, kissing her.

'I expect you must think sometimes I'm a selfish little beast, but I'm not really. At least, I'm not going to be any more.'

'Don't confess any more of your sins, darling,' said Olivia gently, 'or I shall have to confess mine.'

'You? As if you ever—'

Olivia put a hand over the protesting mouth. It was true that George had absolved her; it was an innocent deception, perfectly harmless; but she still felt a little doubtful about it. She would tell him the truth in Paris, on their bit of a honeymoon. Perhaps it would sound more innocent in French.

'I say,' said Dinah suddenly, 'wasn't it lovely about Mr. Pim?'

'Lovely?'

'Yes. Making such a hash of things!'

'Did he make a hash of things?'

'Well, I mean, keeping on coming like that. And if you look at it all round—well, for all he had to say, he needn't really have come at all.'

Indignation on Olympus! The absurdity of the child? Olivia laughed and shook out her curtains—which Mr. Pim had put up.

'Well, I shouldn't quite say that, Dinah,' she murmured.

And now that the curtains are finished at last, what shall we say about them? Personally, I have never been enthusiastic about this particular pair. Nor, I feel, will Olivia retain her enthusiasm for long. She will discover that people are saying, 'What lovely curtains,' instead of 'What a lovely room,' and she will try something else. Perhaps Dinah will get the orange and black ones for her bedroom after all. But, as one of our thinkers observed in an earlier chapter, we must find out our mistakes for ourselves.

'I say, aren't they jolly!' said Dinah. (There you are. They are beginning.)

'I'm so glad everybody likes them,' said Olivia. 'Tell George I'm ready, will you?'

'I say! Is *he* going to hang them up for you?'

He was. Olivia proposed to finish the episode in style. But the style of it was not a matter for discussion with Dinah.

'Well, I thought he could reach best,' she explained.

Dinah accepted the explanation with a smile, and went to the windows to call her uncle. There they were, the two of them, 'walking up and down in order to conceal their emotion,' as she had described them to Mr. Pim that morning, a little prematurely. She called to them, and George waved back from the far end of the terrace.

'Is he coming?' asked Olivia.

'Yes. Brian's just telling him about the five shillings he has got in the Post Office. I expect George was rather surprised to hear about that.'

They came in, George all eagerness.

'Yes, darling?'

'Oh, George dear, just hang these up for me, will you?'

'Of course, darling. I'd better get the steps.'

He hurried into the library. Many were the books in the library; most of them unread; some of them—none the less effective for that—well out of reach. George, however, or one of his ancestors, ever thoughtful for others, had provided a step ladder, by means of which the enthusiast could get into touch with all that was highest in literature. Those steps he seized and bore with him to the morning-room. In a moment he will mount them—perhaps for the first time in his career.

Meanwhile, Brian is introducing himself to his future aunt-in-law, his future wife.

'It's all settled. I'm going to be President of the Royal Academy by next May, and I've promised to paint the front door.'

Olivia smiles happily at him. Dinah rushes up and demands more particulars.

'What did you say to each other? How did you begin? Is he going to give me an allowance? How much money *have* I got?'

'We discussed none of those things. I began by saying "Look here, the whole point is, what am I going to call you? I can't very well call you Marden, and it's absurd to call you Uncle George if Dinah doesn't, and you wouldn't like me to call you George." He agreed that it was very awkward. For a moment we thought that the engagement would fall through. I asked him if he wouldn't consider going into the Church so that I could call him Dean, but he decided against it. Then, just as we were giving up hope, we had a brilliant idea. We decided that I should call him "I say—you—er" for a bit.'

Dinah, laughing, holds out her hand.

'Come on, let's go down to the farm and tell Arnold.'

'Who's Arnold?' asks Olivia.

'Our favourite pig,' Brian explains. 'We shall bring him back with us to see the curtains.'

They laugh their way out of the windows together, the two children.

Then back came George with the steps. The curtains are long, the steps narrow and steep. Just at first it seems that there is going to be an accident, but he achieves the top safely. For a moment he balances there, draped from head to foot in orange and black, Olivia beneath him, looking up anxiously. And in that moment we see Mr. Pim for the last time.

III

We thought we had finished with Mr. Pim. He has said good-bye to George; he has said good-bye to Olivia; he has said good-bye to Dinah and Brian. His letter of introduction to this man Fanshawe has been obtained, his little story about—what was the poor fellow's name—Polwittle—has been told. As he went out of the gate, it seemed that he said goodbye to us too. It might be that we should meet him again some afternoon at Mrs. Brian Strange's, but it was not very probable. For Bloomsbury is indeed farther away from Chelsea than Australia is from England, and an impetuous invitation from Dinah Marden in Buckinghamshire will not bridge the way a year later to Mrs. Strange's London studio. No, we said good-bye to Mr. Pim for ever; we shall never meet (alas!) Miss Prudence Pim.

But we were misjudging our man. Mr. Pim was no puppet of the gods, to be sent to Marden House on a matter of curtains only. Nor was his visit (as Brymer has been thinking) a simple question of a letter of introduction. With some such object he had started out, but the very distressing events of the day had put things in their right perspective for him. Marden House was nothing to him now but the place in which he had mis-told a story. A single error in that story, an error for which he blamed himself entirely, had caused unexpected alarm and anxiety to the household. As soon as he had realized that error, he had hurried back to correct it. The man's name was Henry Polwittle ...

Or was it Ernest?

A small matter. But as we have just seen—as Mr. Pim had just seen—the merest trifle of a misremembered name can threaten disaster to a family. How terrible if he had made yet another mistake! Henry—or was it Ernest?

Twenty yards down the hill he stopped, and looked once more to Heaven for inspiration. If it were Ernest, then his story was still wrong. If it were Ernest, who was Henry Polwittle, this man whose death he had reported so carelessly? He might be anybody ... if it were Ernest.

He followed the man back to Australia; to Sydney; to that morning—how many years ago?—when the poor fellow, just out of prison, had first come to him for help … Now, then, what was the poor fellow's name? Polwittle, of course, yes, but—

And then triumph shone in his old eyes again. What a memory he had! Yes, there was no doubt about it now. He had the story, the whole story, complete, correct, to the minutest detail. What a memory! Eagerly he turned, and made his way back to Marden House.

Olivia, standing by the open windows, saw him coming suddenly. She had no time to wonder why he was here again, no time for more than an instinctive 'H'sh,' whispered finger to mouth. George was at the top of the ladder, visible only as an upheaval of curtain. He could not see, might not hear, Mr. Pim.

Mr. Pim came cautiously nearer. He remembered now that fierce husband of hers, and was in a hurry to be gone. Keeping away from the windows, in case the alarming man was indeed within, he indicated by little jerks of the head that Olivia should come out to him. She looked at George, still enveloped, and moved towards the old gentleman.

'Well?' she breathed.

He would not move his feet; they were near enough to the danger already; but he stretched his head out to her.

'I've just remembered,' he whispered impressively. 'His name was *Ernest* Polwittle—*not* Henry.'

He nodded to her, as much as to say, 'Now it's all right,' and tiptoed away. A minute later he was walking happily down the drive. He had told his story correctly, and was going back with a clear conscience to the Brymers'. For the last time—yes, the last time now—he goes through the gate. Three times it swings backward and forwards behind him, tolling his passing; then with a sudden clatter comes to rest. Mr. Pim has passed by.

Also Available

In his classic autobiography A. A Milne, with his characteristic self-deprecating humour, recalls a blissfully happy childhood in the company of his brothers, and writes with touching affection about the father he adored.

From Westminster School he won a scholarship to Cambridge University where he edited the university magazine, before going out into the world, determined to be a writer. He was assistant editor at *Punch* and went on to enjoy great success with his novels, plays and stories. And of course he is best remembered for his children's novels and verses featuring Winnie-the-Pooh and Christopher Robin.

This is both an account of how a writer was formed and a charming period piece on literary life - Milne met countless famous authors including H. G. Wells, J.M Barrie and Rudyard Kipling.

OUT NOW

Preview

How well can you ever know another person?

Happily married, Reginald and Sylvia seem to lead a perfect, and perfectly quiet, life. They have more than enough money and their own country house. But when success overtakes them, and allure of London life pulls Reginald in, they find parts of themselves they never knew. Where does their happiness really lie?

Reminiscent of Evelyn Waugh, this wry, intimate examination of a relationship is a gem of 1930s literature.

COMING SOON

Preview

Jenny Windell is obsessed with murder mysteries, so when she discovers her estranged aunt dead at her country home, the stage is set for her own investigation.

Worried that being the first at the scene of the crime will make her a suspect and ruin her inquiry, she flees. On the run, she befriends Derek Fenton, the dashing younger brother of acclaimed crime writer Archibald Fenton, and persuades him to join her in her attempts to solve the crime and outsmart dim-witted Inspector Marigold.

An affectionate send-up of the classic Golden Age murder mystery, this charming comedy is A. A. Milne at his most delightful.

COMING SOON

Preview

Chloe Marr is young, beautiful and so irresistible that countless people fall in love with her, and friends are hypnotized by her charm and warmth. Her origins are a mystery and, in London society, such mystique carries both allure and suspicion.

But when an untimely exodus pulls Chloe from the people around her, they soon realise nobody really knows the truth about anybody else…

A. A. Milne's ability to portray interwar society is second to none, and this classic novel of an elusive Mayfair delivers his signature humour and lightness of touch.

COMING SOON

Preview

A new collection of A. A. Milne's short stories and sketches for grown-ups. Collected in full for the first time, they are an epiphany, and show Milne's renowned charm, concision and whimsical flair in all their brilliance.

He paints memorable scenes, from a children's birthday party, to an accidental encounter with murder, and a case of black-mail – often with an unexpected twist. But he also deals in poignancy, from the girl who pulls the wool over her boyfriend's eyes, to a first dance and first disappointment or family reunion and domestic dissonance.

Beguiling and evocative, Milne's thought-provoking stories will make you see his works for children in a whole new light.

COMING SOON

Preview

The Rabbits, as they call themselves, are Archie Mannering, his sister Myra, Samuel Simpson, Thomas of the Admiralty, Dahlia Blair and the narrator, with occasional guests. Their conversation is almost entirely frivolous, their activity vacillates between immensely energetic and happily lazy, and their social mores are surprisingly progressive.

Originally published as sketches in *Punch*, the Rabbits' escapades are a charming portrait of middle-class antics on the brink of being shattered by World War I, and fail entirely to take themselves seriously.

So here they all are. Whatever their crimes, they assure you that they won't do it again – A. A. Milne

COMING SOON

About the Marvellous Milne Series

The Marvellous Milne series brings back to vivid life several of A. A. Milne's classic works for grownups.

Two collections – *The Complete Short Stories*, gathered together in full for the first time; and *The Rabbits* comic sketches, originally published in *Punch* and considered by many to be his most distinctive work – showcase Milne's talent as a short story writer.

Four carefully selected novels – *Four Days' Wonder, Mr Pim, Chloe Marr* and *Two People* – demonstrate his skill across comic genres, from the detective spoof to a timeless and gentle comedy of manners, considering everything from society's relationship with individuals, to intimate spousal relationships.

Alongside this showcase of Milne's talent is his classic memoir *It's Too Late Now*, providing a detailed account of how his writing career was formed, as well as proving a charming period piece of the literary scene at the time.

The full series –
It's Too Late Now
Mr Pim
Two People
Four Days' Wonder
Chloe Marr
The Complete Short Stories
The Rabbits

About the author

A. A. Milne (Alan Alexander) was born in London in 1882 and educated at Westminster School and Trinity College, Cambridge. In 1902 he was Editor of *Granta*, the University magazine, and moved back to London the following year to enter journalism. By 1906 he was Assistant Editor of *Punch*, where he published a series of short stories which now form the collection 'The Rabbits'.

At the beginning of the First World War he joined the Royal Warwickshire Regiment. While in the army in 1917 he started on a career writing plays and novels including *Mr. Pim Passes By, Two People, Four Days' Wonder* and an adaptation of Kenneth Grahame's *The Wind in the Willows* – *Toad of Toad Hall*. He married Dorothy de Selincourt in 1913 and in 1920 had a son, Christopher Robin.

By 1924 Milne was a highly successful playwright, and published the first of his four books for children, a set of poems called *When We Were Very Young*, which he wrote for his son. This was followed by the storybook *Winnie-the-Pooh* in 1926, more poems in *Now We Are Six* (1927) and further stories in *The House at Pooh Corner* (1928).

In addition to his now famous works, Milne wrote many novels, volumes of essays and light verse, works which attracted great success at the time. He continued to be a prolific writer until his death in 1956.

Note from the Publisher

To receive updates on further releases in the Marvellous Milne series – plus special offers and news of other humorous fiction series to make you smile – sign up now to the Farrago mailing list at farragobooks.com/sign-up